BRIDE IN SECRET

by

SERENITY WOODS

Copyright © 2018 Serenity Woods
All rights reserved.
ISBN: 9781719906609

DEDICATION

To Tony & Chris, my Kiwi boys.

CONTENTS

Chapter One 1
Chapter Two 8
Chapter Three 14
Chapter Four 20
Chapter Five 27
Chapter Six 34
Chapter Seven 39
Chapter Eight 45
Chapter Nine 51
Chapter Ten 57
Chapter Eleven 64
Chapter Twelve 70
Chapter Thirteen 77
Chapter Fourteen 83
Chapter Fifteen 89
Chapter Sixteen 95
Chapter Seventeen 102
Chapter Eighteen 108
Chapter Nineteen 114
Chapter Twenty 121
Chapter Twenty-One 128
Chapter Twenty-Two 134
Chapter Twenty-Three 140
Chapter Twenty-Four 146
Newsletter 153
About the Author 154

Chapter One

When she opened her eyes, Roberta's first thought was that she must have been in a car accident. She hurt all over, and her head pounded. Her mouth tasted dry and sour, and her stomach churned. She lay sprawled on her front. Cold air drew light fingers over her bare legs and bottom, although she still appeared to be wearing her favorite black top. Her right arm was twisted at a funny angle, her wrist constrained as if trapped beneath something.

But she rested on a bed, not concrete, a white sheet crumpled and damp beneath her cheek. When she opened her eyes, she saw her phone on the bedside table, along with her earrings, half a glass of water, and… an empty condom packet.

She blinked, ran her tongue across her teeth to encourage some saliva back into her mouth, then lifted her head and looked to her right.

A man lay next to her, on his back. He had short brown hair and a handsome face. Roberta felt a rush of relief that she recognized him, followed quickly by a flood of panic as the reality of the scene struck her. He wore a white shirt that was unbuttoned all the way down, revealing a tanned chest with a scattering of hair. The happy trail on his flat stomach ran beneath the sheet draped over his hips. Quite clearly, he wasn't wearing any underwear, the thin cotton doing nothing to hide an impressive appendage that made her eyes widen.

And now she could see why she couldn't move her right arm. A pair of fur-lined handcuffs linked her right wrist to his.

Holy fuck.

When she tugged on the cuffs, the man stirred, frowned, moistened his lips, then opened his eyes. He blinked a few times at the window, where the open curtains allowed a shaft of sunlight to fall across the room like a gold bar. Lifting his left hand to rub his face, he automatically tried to raise his right hand to match it. On discovering that he couldn't, he turned his head to find out why.

Frozen with mortification and embarrassment, Roberta could only give a weak smile and wait for recognition to dawn on his face.

"Morning, Angus," she said, her voice coming out as a croak.

Dr. Angus McGregor, her brother's mate and a man she would have classed as a good friend until now, blinked. Then, slowly, his gaze slid down her, coming to a stop when it discovered her bare bottom. His eyes widened.

Hurriedly, Roberta pushed up to a sitting position and covered herself with the sheet as he scanned the room. She followed his gaze, taking in the scatter of clothing across the floor, the dozen empty miniature bottles from the mini bar, and the empty condom packet on the bedside table.

Then his gaze came back to hers, and they studied each other for a long, long while.

Roberta couldn't think what to say. Laughter at the ridiculous situation threatened to rise and bubble from her lips, but the look on his face made the giggles dissipate. He did not look amused.

Pushing himself up on the pillows as far as the handcuffs would allow, he cleared his throat and gestured at the condom packet. "Did we… uh…"

"I've no idea," she admitted, somewhat relieved—and a tad insulted—that his memory was as vague as hers.

"What's the last thing you remember?"

She ran a hand through her hair, lifting the mop off her face. They'd come to Las Vegas with a group of her family and friends for a long weekend. Her brother Dominic and his new wife Fliss had spent the first night with them, and then they'd flown on to visit a few other US cities for their honeymoon, while Roberta and the others had remained in Vegas for another two nights. On Saturday, she'd spent the evening with her twin sisters, her other brother, Elliot, and their partners and friends. Last night, they'd all visited the casino, and then everyone else had wanted to go to a show, but she and Angus had been tired, so they'd decided to stay behind and have a drink at the bar before they went to bed.

"I remember going to the bar with you," she said slowly. "We sat at the table in the corner and ordered a couple of whiskies."

"And then a couple more," he said.

"It was fun." She remembered laughing a lot. She'd always liked Angus, and although he'd never seemed interested in her, the more he'd drunk, the more he'd warmed to her, and she'd seen another side of him—friendly, with a wicked sense of humor that had soon turned into sexy flirting. "We went to the nightclub across the road for a while," she added.

He nodded, frowning. "I remember that. It was seventies night, and we danced to disco music. For hours." He flexed his toes. "My feet hurt."

"You did a great John Travolta impersonation," she recalled.

"I don't remember that. I do remember you singing The Nolans' *I'm in the Mood for Dancing.*"

"I don't remember that. Jesus."

"We drank a lot," he said. His lips curved up a fraction. "You dance like a diva."

Snippets of scenes from the night before flitted through her head like scraps of paper tossed into the air. Songs from the night club— *Night Fever, Dancing Queen, Boogie Wonderland*. Angus twirling her about, the two of them spinning, moving together better than she'd expected—he'd had all the moves. Dancing to a few slow songs, giggling together at the words, *If I Said You Had a Beautiful Body Would You Hold it Against Me?* Angus pretending to grope her butt, her squealing with laughter. More whisky. And then… her arms around his neck, his around her waist… Slipping her fingers through his short hair… His lips grazing her cheek, then finally her mouth, his tongue sliding against hers…

His warm eyes suggested he was recalling the same thing. "You were a lot of fun."

She lifted her right hand, bringing his with it, and stared at the handcuffs. Her body heated. What the hell had they gotten up to?

"We need to look for a key," he said. His smile had disappeared, a frown replacing it again. "We're flying out today, and I don't think they'll let us board like this."

"Oh shit, yeah." Her heart picked up its pace at the thought of the others discovering what had happened.

They both glanced around. "This is my room," he said, gesturing at the suitcase in the corner. His boxers lay across it like a flag claiming possession.

Her gaze slid back to his crotch. The thin cotton sheet hid nothing from view.

"Hey." He snatched a pillow and brought it over himself.

"We obviously made out," she stated. "It's a bit late to be coy."

"Maybe we didn't get down to anything. We probably fell asleep. I'm sure I'd have remembered if we'd…" He waved his free hand.

"The condom packet's empty," she pointed out.

"Still doesn't prove anything." His gaze slid to where she clutched the sheet between her thighs. "Can you tell if we…"

Her face burned. "Seriously?"

"Want me to check? I am a doctor."

"Angus! This isn't a laughing matter."

"Do I look like I'm smiling?" He wasn't, although she was certain he was teasing her.

She blew out a breath. "Close your eyes."

He did so. Glaring at him, she slid a hand down under the sheet, between her legs, and felt around.

"Well?" he asked.

"I don't know," she said impatiently, removing her hand. "It's not clear."

He opened his eyes. "Is there… moisture?"

"There's always moisture. I'm a moist person."

His lips twitched. "Any… soreness?"

"No."

"Maybe I was just very gentle."

Her face burned again. "You're getting far too much fun out of this."

"Did you check everywhere?" he wanted to know. "Just in case we…"

Was he referring to anal sex? "If you're talking about what I think you're talking about, I don't know whether to be flattered or insulted!"

His eyes gleamed. "Well, we were drunk."

"I could never be that drunk!"

"Maybe I was very persuasive." He was laughing now, obviously relieved that the evidence pointed to them abstaining. When she glared at him, he grinned and tugged his right arm across his body, causing her to lean across him. "Come here," he said, pulling her into his arms. "And stop worrying. Look, the condom's there." He pointed to where it lay half-hidden beneath his wallet on the bedside table, unused. "We obviously fell asleep. Nothing happened."

"Unless we did it without a condom…"

His eyes widened. "I wouldn't have…"

"Even drunk?"

"Jeez, Roberta."

"I think it's all right. There's no sign of your… you know…" She gestured between her legs.

They both blew out a breath, and then started laughing.

"Holy fuck." She sighed. "I can't believe we nearly did it."

"Hmm." He smiled. Wow, he was gorgeous. Part of her wished they *had* done it, even if she couldn't remember it. It would be nice to believe she'd been wanted by a man like this.

"It was a fun evening," she said. "It's just a shame that you had to be out of your tree to like me."

He blinked. "What?"

"You were different last night. Normally, you're very cool to me. I thought you didn't like me much."

His expression softened. "I like you a lot. That's not why…" His voice trailed off, and he leaned forward and tugged at a piece of paper caught beneath the sheet. "What's that?"

She lifted her knee so he could retrieve it. He picked it up with his left hand and brought it up to study it.

After about ten seconds, his gaze came back to hers.

"What is it?" she asked, starting to feel alarmed at the lack of expression on his face.

He held the paper out to her, and she took it and turned it over.

At the top it said, quite clearly, Marriage Certificate. Underneath the fancy header, it declared that Roberta Karen Goldsmith and Angus Hamish McGregor had joined 'in lawful wedlock' on the seventh day of July. There was a picture of Elvis in the corner.

Fucking hell. She'd gone and married the dude while she was plastered. And not only that, she'd done it in an Elvis wedding chapel.

She lowered the certificate to the bed. "Huh."

His smile had vanished. "Do you think it's real?"

She swallowed hard. "It looks it."

"Christ," he said. "We must have gone to one of those walk-in places."

She brushed a finger over the picture of Elvis. "Do you think they played *Love Me Tender* while we walked up the aisle?" She pursed her lips at the look on his face. "Or maybe *Crying in the Chapel*." To her shame, tears pricked her eyes. It was funny, wasn't it? Hell, they'd both gotten drunk. It was just a stupid mistake. They should be laughing about it. Did he have to look so horrified?

"Do you remember it at all?" she whispered.

"I don't remember anything after the night club." His gaze slid to her mouth. "Not much, anyway." He remembered kissing her, then.

They both fell silent. Roberta's head was spinning, partly from her raging hangover, partly from the news that, only hours ago, she'd promised to love this man for the rest of her life. Just words. And yet…

"Who were the witnesses?" she asked.

He read the names from the certificate. "Mark Lennon and Anna Mc… something. I can't read the handwriting."

"Never heard of them," she admitted.

"They must have been passersby."

Her heart raced. She'd known this man a long time, but until now she'd never even kissed him, let alone pledged the rest of eternity to him.

It didn't matter that they'd been drunk. That they didn't remember it. Or that it had probably been done by an Elvis impersonator. The services carried out in Vegas were legal and binding. They were married.

Angus's eyes burned into hers, a bright blue. She'd always liked him, right from the first moment they'd met, nearly two years ago, when her brother, Elliot, had introduced them. A GP at the local doctor's surgery, Angus was in his early thirties, tall, well-built, and gorgeous. His boyish features and smooth jaw made him look younger than his age, but she knew he'd travelled extensively and had worked in Europe for a while.

He was a difficult guy to get to know—he didn't talk much about himself, and carefully side-stepped any questions about his private life. She had no doubt that most of his female patients and probably some of the male ones too were half in love with him. But she'd never seen him with a woman or heard of him dating anyone. At weekends, he often disappeared to Auckland, prompting Elliot to tease him that he had a girl down there, but he always insisted he was visiting family, and he had a manner about him that prevented her from asking for more details.

Roberta had assumed that she was too loud for him, that he didn't fancy her, or that maybe he'd lied to Elliot and did have a girl in Auckland. Whatever the reason, she'd crossed him off her list of possibilities for a partner, even if she'd secretly daydreamed about having a fling with him.

And now they were married.

It was horrifying news, she told herself firmly. They'd been so drunk that they didn't even remember getting hitched. It was hardly the romantic event she'd always dreamed of, especially working in her family business, the Bay of Islands Brides. There had been no touching ceremony, no beautiful dress. Angus hadn't chosen her, and he wasn't in love with her. The piece of paper didn't mean anything.

And yet they were married by law. He'd promised to love and cherish her for the rest of his life, and she'd done the same.

Till death parts us.

Warmth spread through her, and she dropped her gaze to his mouth. If she leaned forward and kissed him now, what would he do?

Chapter Two

The fog was finally clearing.

This wasn't a dream his subconscious had created for him from which he could wake. And it wasn't some fantasy he'd conjured up while sitting in a boring meeting at the surgery.

He—Angus McGregor, Doctor of Medicine, a respected General Practitioner—had gotten completely off his face, seduced—or tried to seduce—the very woman he knew he shouldn't go anywhere near, and then he'd… holy fucking hell… he'd gone and married her.

What had he been thinking? Forget equality and the fact that Roberta was always telling everyone she could look after herself—he'd promised Elliot when the rest of the gang went off to the show that he'd look after her and make sure she got back to her room safely. He'd fully intended to fulfil that role. When she'd asked him if he fancied a drink in the bar before going to their rooms, he'd thought: well, what harm could there be in that? One drink, a chance to spend some time alone with her, to make her laugh, and to watch the dimples appear in her cheeks. To admire her from afar. But the one drink had turned into two, and Roberta had come alive, teasing him, laughing, flirting, her eyes alight with life, promising a short period of relief from the weight of the world he carried on his shoulders.

The two drinks had turned into four, and then they'd decided to go dancing… She'd been light on her feet, a joy to spin around the club. He loved disco, and he'd enjoyed every minute of their time together, singing to all the old songs, strutting his stuff on the dance floor. What could another whisky matter? They'd had such fun that he hadn't wanted the evening to end.

But at some point, the alcohol had sunk its insidious claws into his inhibitions and ripped them away. The small part of his brain that kept warning him to keep aloof had been outvoted by the part that had wanted Roberta since that first day he'd met her. And even though he knew he mustn't take advantage of her, that she was inebriated and no more in control of what she wanted than he was, when they'd danced together her body had been soft and her eyes glittering, and he'd been unable to fight the urge to press his lips to hers.

He was such a fucking lightweight. When he was young, he'd never been able to hold his drink the same way some of his friends had. They'd be onto their fifth pint and he'd be on his back on a bench in the bar, already asleep. It had been a standing joke. So why had he thought he'd be different last night?

He hadn't cared. That was the problem. He'd wanted to kiss her for ages, and last night she'd looked stunning in her black top and her tight jeans, her long brown hair loose for once, flowing over her shoulders like melted chocolate. Now, it was all mussed, and she looked bleary eyed and hungover, but she was still gorgeous, and his fingers itched to reach out and touch the bare hip that jutted out above the white sheet. He wished he could remember stripping the jeans off her. Had he kissed her pale skin as he'd pulled them down her thighs? Had he buried his mouth in her and given her pleasure? Or had he passed out before he could bring himself to do even that?

God, he was disgusted with himself. He'd been irresponsible, and Elliot was going to fucking kill him.

Holy shit. Elliot!

"What time is it?" When she shook her head, he turned to pick up his phone, pressed the button on the side, and blew out a breath. "It's nearly seven thirty. We're meeting the guys at eight, right?"

"Yeah."

He put the phone down and turned back to her. Her eyes were warm, and she was looking at his lips as if... oh no... as if she was thinking about kissing him. He had to put a stop to this right now.

He ran a hand through his hair again. "I'm so sorry about all this." He gestured at the bed. "I apologize for being so... ungentlemanly."

Her lips twitched. "Ungentlemanly?"

"I should have been more responsible."

"Responsible?" A look of impatience flitted across her features. "Angus, I'm twenty-eight. Not eighteen. I got drunk too."

"Yeah, but I'm the guy here."

"Where are you from, the eighteen-thirties? This isn't Regency England. This is twenty-first-century New Zealand. Well, okay, we're in Vegas at the moment, but you know what I mean."

"Yes, but—"

"The only person here responsible for what I did last night currently has hair like a banshee and a cold butt."

"I didn't think my hair was that bad," he tried to joke.

She glared at him. "I knew perfectly well what I was doing when I drank the first whisky, and the second, and the rest of them. I knew what I was doing when we danced, and… when we kissed." Her gaze had dropped to his mouth again.

"How can you be responsible for what happened afterward if you can't remember it?" he asked softly.

"How can you?"

"That's not the point."

"What is the point?"

"It was a mistake," he said, somewhat irritably. "A terrible mistake."

The light faded from her eyes. "I see."

Shit. Now she thought he was regretting what they'd done. Well, he was. Wasn't he? Of course he was. There was no way he'd have gone to that chapel with her if he'd been sober. The absolute last thing he would have wanted was to marry her.

"Look," he said, "I had a great evening, but it went much too far."

She studied his face, and then gave a slow nod. "Of course."

"I'm not saying I didn't have fun—"

"I know what you're saying, Angus. And you're right. It was stupid to get so drunk."

He was relieved she agreed with him. "The last thing I want is to spoil our friendship." He meant it. Both Roberta and the rest of her family were precious to him, and he'd have been horrified if losing control last night had meant spoiling that relationship.

"Of course not," she said softly. "That's the last thing I want, too."

"Okay, well, we'd better try to find the key to these." He lifted the handcuffs. "Or we're going to have Elliot knocking on the door asking me if I've seen you."

"Yeah, I didn't think of that."

She went to get up, and so did he, on opposite sides of the bed. They quickly realized that wasn't going to work.

"I'll come to your side," she said, and scooted across. The sheet over her midriff rose as she moved, revealing her long, slender legs, a smooth hip, and a flash of her tummy leading down to some very pale skin…

"Angus!"

He tore his gaze away as she snatched the sheet over her again. "Sorry." He gestured at his case in the corner. "Let me put my boxers on, and I can drop the sheet then." He stood and sidled over to the case, Roberta shuffling across the bed with him, and retrieved his underwear. He slid the boxers on, relieved they were one of his better pairs and not the baggy gray ones he wore when everything else was in the wash.

Roberta took great care to look the other way, only returning her gaze as he dropped the sheet. He saw her scan the boxers and his thighs, and noticed a flush appear in her cheeks as she did so.

"I'm hot," she said when she realized he'd noticed.

Hiding a smile, he picked up a pair of tiny white panties. "I'm guessing these are yours."

She took them, mumbling under her breath, and slid her legs through them. He made sure to look the other way as she pulled them up, even though it took great effort to avert his gaze. How he wished he could remember going to bed with her last night. He'd touched that soft skin, stroked down her back and over her bottom to her silky thighs. Had he stroked her, slid his fingers into her, he wondered again? Had she moaned at his touch?

She straightened, then did a double take at his crotch. Only then did he realize he had an erection.

"I need to pee," he said. He was only half lying.

She cleared her throat. "Right. Actually, so do I. Christ! We need to find that key."

They spent ten minutes searching the room. It was difficult chained up, and with both of them bleary eyed and hungover. They looked through their discarded clothing, in their pockets, under the bed, but couldn't find it.

A touch of panic lit Roberta's eyes. "What are we going to do?"

This was starting not to be funny anymore. "Okay," he said, "one step at a time. I really need to pee and I'm sure you do, too."

"I'm not peeing with you in the room, Angus McGregor."

"I'll try to stand outside. Or do you want to hold it until we reach Auckland?"

Grumbling under her breath, she followed him to the bathroom. They stood in the doorway and studied the room. It was a decent size, and the toilet was tucked in the corner, on the opposite side to the door. Angus stood in the middle and turned his back to the toilet. There were mirrors everywhere. He'd be able to see her from wherever he stood.

Roberta picked up a towel. "Put this over your head."

"Are you serious?"

"Look at my face."

He studied her expression, then draped the towel over his head.

"And close your ears," she warned.

"How am I supposed to do that?"

"Well, just don't listen."

"All right. I'm not listening."

He felt her move across to the toilet, her arm outstretched to keep him as far away as she could. There was a rustle of flimsy underwear, and she lowered herself down.

Angus began whistling, and she started to laugh.

"I cannot believe I'm in this situation," she said.

"I am sorry. From the bottom of my heart."

"What are we going to do?" she whispered.

"We'll have another search for the key in a minute."

"I meant about the marriage certificate."

He heard the flush go and waited until she'd risen and given him permission to look, and then he removed the towel from his head. "Let's worry about that later. One step at a time."

She nodded and gestured at the toilet, took the towel from him, and draped it over her mussed brown hair.

"This isn't easy," he grumbled. "I usually hold it with my right hand."

"Please don't. And if you feel the need to do anything else with your right hand, I'd appreciate it if you fought the urge until we find the key."

He gave a short laugh and flushed the toilet. She removed the towel from her head, and together they went over to the sink and washed their hands.

They had to stand close together because their right hands were linked. Angus looked down at her as they let the warm water run over their skin. She'd drawn her hair over her left shoulder, leaving her neck bare, and his gaze lingered on the light-brown skin there, which he knew would be soft beneath his lips. She spent a lot of time outside in her garden, working on her vegetable patch. Her arms were tanned, and a line around her upper arms beneath the capped sleeves of the black top showed where she usually wore a T-shirt. He was a few inches taller than her, and the deep V-neck of the top led his gaze down to the paler skin of the swell of her breasts. She was still wearing her bra, so he obviously hadn't managed to extricate it last night.

Her face had flushed, and he raised an eyebrow as she reached for the towel and met his gaze in the mirror.

"I was just wondering what we got up to last night," she said. She lifted her right arm and indicated the cuffs. "Do you think you were trying to handcuff me to the bed and missed?"

Angus smiled, but he knew why he would have chained himself to her. In his drunken stupor, he would have been so thrilled to finally get his hands on her that he would have thought the cuffs would make sure she never left.

For nearly two years, he'd kept his distance from this girl because, of all the women he'd met since moving to the Northland, she was the only one who fascinated him, and who made his heart beat faster. And therefore the only one with whom he absolutely couldn't afford to get involved.

What an idiot.

Chapter Three

Angus was staring at her with a stony look on his face, and Roberta had the feeling he was wishing he was anywhere else but in the hotel room at that moment. She swallowed hard, fighting against the urge to burst into tears like a two-year-old. Okay, so he'd been drunk last night and this was all a mistake—he didn't have to act quite so cross.

"We'd better have another look for the key," she said, dropping her gaze.

"Right."

In silence, they searched the bathroom, then returned to the bedroom, dropping to their hands and knees to search.

"Got it!" Angus's voice was filled with relief, and he emerged from beneath the bedside table with the key in his hand.

The two of them sat on the floor with their backs to the bed, and Angus took her right hand in his left. "Let's do you first," he said.

"Is that what you said last night?" She waited for him to laugh, but although his lips curved up a fraction, he didn't smile.

Her throat tightened. He really didn't find this funny. He was a GP, a respected member of the community, and he must be worried that people were going to find out what they'd done. He was right—they'd been irresponsible. They weren't teenagers who'd gone out on their first night of freedom and gotten drunk because they didn't understand the effects of alcohol. They were adults who should have known better.

It didn't matter as much to her because she didn't care what people thought, and she liked him, and it gave her a warm fuzzy feeling to think that when he'd let his guard down, he'd seemed to like her a lot. But clearly Angus was a man who didn't give in to his passions. When sober, he didn't consider her a suitable proposition, and he obviously had no interest in pursuing a relationship with her. That stung, but she could either weep and wail about it and make a fool of herself, or accept that she'd made a mistake and deal with it, using as much dignity as she could muster.

It wouldn't be the first time. She should be used to this feeling of humiliation by now.

Angus was making no attempt to unlock her, and she had the feeling he was trying to think how to explain what he was feeling. Not wanting to hear him talk about what a big mistake it was again, she decided to help him out.

"I'm sorry," she said in a low voice. "I shouldn't make light of it. I should have been more responsible—we both should have been. We'll deal with the certificate thing when we get home. I'm guessing we can get an annulment or something? Or will we have to apply for a divorce?"

"I'm not sure."

"Well, we'll sort it out. And we won't tell anyone what happened."

The muscles moved at the corners of his jaw, suggesting he was clenching his teeth. Was he angry with her? Or just at the situation?

"Don't be angry with me," she whispered, hating that she sounded pathetic but unable to bear it.

His eyebrow rose. "I'm not. Of course I'm not. I'm angry with myself for putting us both in this situation."

"It's all right. Nobody needs to know. I won't even tell Elliot, I swear. I'll be a bride in secret." She gave a weak smile.

His gaze slid to her mouth, and she reacted instinctively, moistening her lips with the tip of her tongue. He watched her, his gaze sliding slowly down. She followed it, seeing it resting on where her legs were curled beneath her, her tanned skin shining in the light. Was he thinking about where he'd touched her last night? She wished she could remember what had happened. Had they taken off their pants and immediately crashed out? Or had they lain in bed for a while, stroking, touching, kissing? Could she remember his hot mouth, his tongue sliding against hers, his deep groans as her hand sought him out beneath the duvet? Was it her imagination, or had he stroked over her stomach and down between her legs, his fingers sliding into her swollen folds, encouraging her to a sleepy climax before they'd passed out?

She looked up into his bright blue eyes. His expression held regret, not desire, as she'd hoped. Her heart sank, and she squashed the feelings spiraling inside her.

With any other man, she might have gotten angry at his obvious wish that none of this had happened. Told him that she was sick of being someone's mistake—again. But he was Elliot's friend and they all saw each other a lot socially, and she didn't want to upset the group dynamics. She was as much to blame for what had happened as he was. He hadn't seduced her. She'd wanted this, and she was ashamed of how she'd behaved.

"I don't want to embarrass you," she said quietly.

His frown lifted at that, and he lifted his left hand to cup her face. "Sweetheart, you could never do that. I'm so sorry. I wish—"

But she was never to find out what he wished, because at that moment someone knocked on the door and shouted, "Angus! Are you up yet, you lazy bastard?"

It was Elliot.

"I'm up," Angus yelled back, inserting the key in the lock of the handcuffs and twisting. It popped open, and she released her wrist, rubbing the skin where the fake fur had worn free and the metal had rubbed against her. "I overslept. I'll be down in five."

"Can you knock on Roberta's door on the way?" Elliot asked. "She's obviously crashed out. See if you can wake her up."

Angus glanced at her. "Will do. I'll see you down there." Footsteps sounded going away from the door.

They both blew out a breath. Angus unlocked the cuffs from his own wrist, and together they rose and searched out their clothing. He buttoned up his shirt and they both pulled on their jeans. She stuffed her feet in her Converses, fighting against tears that pricked her eyes. She was twenty-eight, due be twenty-nine in a month's time, heading toward thirty at a rate of knots. She should have found her Mr. Right by now. Flirty dates at university, a couple of partners in her early twenties, then finding the right man around twenty-four or twenty-five, a year of dating, a couple of years living together, and then marriage and the first baby on the way by the time she turned the big three-oh. That was how it should have happened. Instead, she'd thrown away her early twenties betting on a horse that had left the gate but stumbled at the first hurdle, a horse that she should have known was never going to reach the finishing line. And now here she was again, with another man who had no interest in her, getting drunk and sleeping around as if she had no self-respect at all. She was disgusted with herself.

Grabbing her purse, she gestured to the door. "Can you check that the corridor's empty? I'll go back to my room for ten minutes and freshen up."

Angus nodded and went over to the door. She joined him there, waiting for him to open it. When he didn't, she looked up to see him watching her, his brow furrowed.

"I—" he began.

"Don't." Her voice was harsh.

He didn't finish the sentence, his mouth thinning. "I'll see you downstairs." She nodded. He opened the door a crack, then peeked out. "It's empty."

Not looking at him, Roberta slipped past, trying not to brush against him. Once in the corridor, she ran down to the other end, found her room, inserted her key card, and went inside.

When she got there, she took a deep shaky breath and blew it out slowly. As far as she knew, nobody had seen them.

Emotion washed over her, but she dashed her tears away angrily. There was no point in getting upset. Nothing had happened; it wasn't as if they'd slept together in the end. It had been a stupid mistake, and she was going to have to suck it up and deal with it. She'd just pretend it hadn't happened. She and Angus had had a fun evening, enjoyed a couple of drinks and a dance, and then had returned to their own separate rooms. That would be their story, and they wouldn't have to explain anything to anyone.

On the seventh day of July, Roberta Karen Goldsmith and Angus Hamish McGregor joined 'in lawful wedlock'...

She covered her face with her hands and sank onto her bed, thinking of her older brother, Dominic. He was an ordained deacon, and although not a priest, he was a man of God who had performed the marriage when her sister married her own husband. Dominic himself had only just gotten married to Fliss, an actress and her old school friend, who'd come to stay with her for a while. What would he say if he knew what Roberta had done? If he knew what a mockery she'd made of the institution of marriage?

She sank her hands into her hair. She and Angus hadn't gotten married in church. They hadn't taken their vows before God. It might have been legally binding, but it wasn't the same. Dominic might roll his eyes if he were to find out what they'd done, but he wouldn't judge her too harshly—he wasn't like that.

A tear rolled down her cheek, and she bit her lip. It didn't matter what she thought Dominic might say. She had always viewed marriage as something precious that should be treated with respect. Not as a piece of paper that could be dismissed with a simple appeal, like paying off a parking ticket. It didn't matter that it hadn't been held in a church. If she and Angus had been in love, getting married in Vegas on a whim would have been fun and romantic, and everyone would have been thrilled for them. But doing what they'd done had been childish and foolish. They were both to blame, and they should be ashamed at their actions.

Slowly, she got to her feet and went into the bathroom. She had a sixteen-hour flight before her, and she'd rather skip breakfast than go downstairs the mess she was right now. She looked into the mirror, staring in disgust at her panda eyes, her wild hair, her blotchy skin. Man, she looked scary. No wonder Angus had seemed so alarmed at the thought of tying the knot with her.

After ripping off her clothes, she set the shower to scalding and scrubbed her skin and hair, wishing she could erase the memories of the night with it. When her skin was pink and raw, she got out and dried herself, blow-dried her hair, and braided it tightly. She didn't apply any makeup and dressed in a clean shirt and jeans. Afterward, she examined herself in the mirror. She looked pale, her scraped-back hair making her look harsh and unattractive. But that was good. It was what she deserved.

She gathered her things together, repacked her suitcase, stood it by the door, and then finally left the room and went downstairs.

The rest of the gang were in the dining room, finishing off their breakfast. They cheered as she came in, and she gave them a weak smile. Angus was already there, talking to Elliot. She felt his gaze on her as she took a seat a few chairs down, but she didn't look at him.

"Hey you," her sister, Phoebe, said. "You're late. You feeling all right?"

"A bit worse for wear. I drank too much last night."

Phoebe's twin sister, Bianca, smirked and gestured at Angus. "I understand the two of you had some sort of whisky drinking game."

"Who won?" Rafe wanted to know.

"Um… It's not clear," Angus said, making them all laugh.

Elliot snorted. "You've never been able to hold your drink. I bet you had one whisky and you were under the table." They all looked at Roberta for confirmation.

"Let's just say that I've discovered he can moonwalk better than Michael Jackson," she said, causing more laughter to erupt.

Angus met her eyes then and gave her a rueful smile.

"Oh, I wish I could have seen that," Libby, their good friend, said.

"You didn't miss much," Roberta mumbled, nodding when Libby's partner, Mike, offered her some coffee. She drank it black and unsweetened, telling herself she didn't deserve sugar and cream.

"I hope Dominic and Fliss are having a good time," Bianca said with a sigh.

"Where are they off to next?" Libby asked.

"Um… New York, I think." The conversation continued. Nobody commented on anything that had happened the night before. It looked as if they'd escaped detection.

Roberta put her cup in her saucer, sadness overwhelming her. Was it odd that a part of her wished she and Angus had been seen? That they'd then be able to talk about going to the chapel, and what it meant? The secrecy only made it all feel even more sleazy and sordid, if that were possible.

Flicking a glance across at Angus, she caught him watching her, his expression carefully blank, but when he saw her looking the corner of his mouth quirked up and his eyes softened.

She looked away. She just wanted to go home now, to her house in the country, to her cats and her painting and her cooking, and to working in the lovely Bridal Café. To the life she'd made for herself. She didn't need a man to make it complete. She was doing perfectly well on her own.

If she said it often enough, maybe she'd begin to believe it.

Chapter Four

The airport was bustling, full of bright lights and loud announcements. Angus had taken two Panadol, but his head ached and his stomach churned. He wasn't sure if it was from the drink or the thought of what had happened the night before. Probably a combination of both.

Roberta hadn't spoken to him since she'd left his room that morning. He couldn't blame her. She'd kept to herself, telling everyone she had a hangover, and sat a few seats away, reading something on her phone. He was tempted to sit next to her, but he couldn't think what he could possibly say to make things better, and he wasn't sure if she'd talk to him anyway. So he stayed put, flicked through his emails on his phone, and tried to ignore the voice in his head that had seen the hurt in Roberta's eyes, reminding him what an idiot he'd been.

Luckily, the flight wasn't delayed, and before long they boarded the plane. It was a short, uneventful flight to LA, where they then changed planes for the longer flight to Auckland.

Fliss had made the booking and had grouped them all together. In the smaller plane, he'd sat next to Bianca, but it was only when they arrived at their seats in the bigger plane, which were in rows of three, that he realized his was an aisle seat next to Roberta's, who was in the middle, with Bianca by the window.

He stopped and glanced at Elliot, who was stuffing his bag in the overhead locker opposite him. "Want to change seats?"

"Why?" Elliot moved back to let Karen squeeze in past him.

"Roberta's not feeling great and I take up too much room," Angus said weakly. At six-two and with wide shoulders, he frequently intruded into his neighbor's seat, and he didn't think she would appreciate that.

"I'm not exactly skinny," Elliot said, ducking under the locker and sliding into his own seat. "Sit down and stop making a fuss."

Angus mumbled under his breath, put his rucksack in the locker, and then lowered himself down. "Sorry about this," he mumbled, making a nuisance of himself as he tried to extricate one end of the seatbelt from beneath his butt, elbowing her in the process.

She didn't answer. He fumbled with the belt, connected the two ends, then sat back.

This plane was part of a brand-new series, with bright, clean upholstery and smart TV screens showing the latest movies. He had long legs and on other airlines had to sit bolt upright to make sure he had enough room to fit his knees in, but here there was plenty of room for him to stretch out. However, at that moment he wished the economy seat was a few inches bigger. His thigh pressed against Roberta's, and his upper arm overlapped hers. He was sure it was the last thing she wanted.

She didn't complain, though, she just swiped the screen of her phone with her thumb, not looking up.

"What are you reading?" he asked.

She glanced at Bianca, obviously decided it would look weird if she refused to talk to him, and said, "A biography of Monet."

His eyebrows rose. "I didn't know you were interested in art."

"There are a lot of things you don't know about me."

It was a put down, and he supposed he deserved it, although it puzzled him. She'd admitted her part in the evening and had stated that it had all been a mistake. Why was she angry with him now? A little irritated, he decided to keep to himself for the rest of the flight. Let her speak to Bianca and ignore him if she wanted.

They went through the safety talk as the plane started to taxi down the runway, and then they took off, heading west across the Pacific.

Angus put on his headphones, stuck on the latest Bourne movie, ate the breakfast the attendant delivered, and occasionally chatted to Elliot across the aisle. Roberta also put on her headphones and watched a movie as she ate her food. Eating was like a kind of dance, trying to open the small pots and lifting the forks to their mouths without bumping each other.

It was a long flight, and he dozed for a while, trying not to think about the warmth of her arm, the softness of her thigh pressed to his. It wouldn't do him any good to dwell on the vision of her when he'd awoken that morning, her hair mussed, her bare legs leading his gaze up to the swell of her naked bottom, which had looked soft and flawless in the early morning light.

He shifted in the seat, causing her to grumble under her breath.

"Sorry," he muttered.

"There's too much of you," she stated, poking at where his arm overlapped hers.

"Not a complaint I usually have."

She rolled her eyes and removed her headphones.

"Not even a smile?" he asked.

Her eyes met his briefly. All the Goldsmiths had green eyes, but Roberta's were a deeper shade than her brothers' and sisters', a dark forest-green, with flecks of gold at the center.

"I'm sorry," he said, even though he wasn't sure what he was apologizing for. He just wanted her to like him again.

Her gaze slid to Bianca, who was looking out of the window, then back again. She gave a little shake of her head. What did that mean? Don't talk about it? Don't worry about it?

He tucked his headphones in the pocket in front of him. In another world, he would have apologized for his behavior the night before and offered to take her out to dinner to make up for it. Used it as an excuse to date her properly. But he couldn't do that.

He wouldn't change anything about his circumstances, but he wished he could say something to Roberta to explain that the reason he regretted what had happened wasn't because he didn't like her. Last night, she'd looked up at him with desire in her eyes as they'd danced, and for a few hours he'd had fun imagining they were really a couple. No wonder his subconscious had delighted in being given the liberty to do what it wanted with her for a while.

"That's weird," Bianca said.

He glanced across, seeing Roberta do the same. "What?" they both asked.

Bianca pointed at the plane's engine, on the wing in front of them. "I thought I saw..." She inhaled sharply, and the two of them exclaimed as yellow tongues of flames licked out from the engine.

"Fuck." He exchanged a glance with Roberta. The alarm in her eyes reflected his own.

Angus glanced across the plane, wondering whether to call the flight attendant.

"What is it?" Elliot had heard his exclamation and obviously spotted their alarm.

Angus leaned across, beckoning for Elliot to do the same. He didn't want everyone hearing what he was about to say.

"The engine's on fire," he whispered. His heart raced.

Elliot stared at him.

"Other people are going to notice soon," Angus pointed out.

Elliot, ever the police officer, nodded, unclipped his belt, and rose out of his seat. He made his way to where the attendants were in the galley preparing a meal and drew the curtain across. After a short time, he came back out, the attendant following him. She came over to his seat and bent as if to talk to Angus, but looked out at the engine.

Then she glanced down and met Angus's eyes. Her instinctive smile did nothing to allay his fears. "Nothing to worry about, sir," she said. Straightening, she walked purposefully back through to the galley. He was pretty sure she was going down to speak to the captain.

Elliot came back to his seat and buckled himself back in. He glanced at Angus, then turned to whisper to Karen.

"Jesus," Roberta muttered. Angus followed her gaze and saw more flames engulfing the engine. Holy fuck. "How serious is it?" she murmured.

"I don't know. Engine fires happen. They shut off the fuel and use an in-built fire extinguisher. We can fly on one engine, but I imagine they'd still land at the nearest airport."

"We're over the Pacific Ocean," she said. "Not a lot of land around here."

He tapped on the screen in front of him and brought up the flight plan. "There are loads of islands around. Look, we're not far from Rarotonga, and they have a decent airfield. Maybe we'll land there."

Behind them, Mike—Libby's partner—leaned forward and poked Angus's shoulder. "What's going on?" His gaze followed Roberta's. "Holy shit!" His jaw dropped, and he whispered furiously to Libby, sitting by the window.

Elliot—who'd never liked Mike much—glared over his shoulder at him, but it was too late; the cat was out of the bag. People started moving, craning their necks, exclaiming as they saw the fire.

At that moment, the speaker crackled and the captain started speaking. "Ladies and gentlemen, if I could have your attention please. As some of you have noticed, we appear to have a small fire in the engine on the right side of the plane. We are attempting to control it, but we have reported it in the event that we have to make an emergency landing. At this time, please remain in your seats with your seatbelts on, and follow the instructions of the flight crew. I'll let you know as soon as we have any further information."

The noise level rose in the cabin, and the flight attendants moved down the aisles, attempting to quieten and console the passengers.

"Please don't worry," the attendant nearest them said, "we're taking precautions to control the problem. Please stay in your seats and remain calm."

Angus exchanged a glance with Elliot and saw his own worries mirrored in his friend's eyes.

"How low are we?" Elliot asked.

Angus craned his neck to look across the girls at the ground beneath them, seeing clouds out of the window. "Still high. Thirty thousand feet?"

Elliot turned to Karen, patting her hand and reassuring her as the attendant moved through the cabin, doing the same in a calm voice.

Angus looked at Roberta. "Don't bullshit me," she said. "This is bad, isn't it?"

He glanced at Bianca, seeing both of them pale but composed. Neither of them would want platitudes. "It's not good," he said. He wished he could come up with something to make it better, to put their minds at rest, but there was nothing to say.

He could feel pressure on his ears; the plane was starting to descend. As the thought entered his head, so the speaker crackled again. "Ladies and gentlemen, unfortunately we are having trouble extinguishing the engine fire, so we're going to land at the nearest airport and address the issue. Rarotonga Airport have cleared us for landing, so please stay in your seats and flight crew, prepare for landing. If—"

A loud bang interrupted his words, and Angus watched in horror as pieces of metal peeled away from the engine like a body being stripped of its skin.

"Fuck," Roberta said as the plane shuddered. "What happened?"

"It's coming apart," Bianca said, her voice holding a hint of panic.

Angus's eyes were glued to the fiery engine. The plane was descending rapidly. They couldn't be far from Rarotonga. The ground crew would be gathering their emergency services, preparing for the landing. But what if they couldn't land? What if they couldn't make the runway? Angus's heart thundered and his mouth had gone dry. Behind him, he could hear children crying, picking up on their parents' fear. Oh God, there were two babies on the plane, lots of kids… The flight assistants moved between them, offering blankets and cushions, trying to comfort, to reassure.

The speakers crackled, and the pilot spoke again. "Well, ladies and gentlemen, as you probably heard, there has been a small explosion in the engine that has affected our flight controls, and we're descending faster than we should. We're closing in on Rarotonga, but in case we can't reach the airport, we'll try landing on the eastern side of the island."

While the pilot continued to talk, telling them to put on their oxygen masks as they dropped from the ceiling and prepare for an emergency landing, Angus glanced at Elliot, then further along at Rafe, who was leaning across to see how the girls were doing. All three of the guys, as well as Mike, were used to working under pressure. Elliot and Mike, the police officers, and Rafe, the firefighter, attended the scenes of accidents on a regular basis, and Angus had done a rotation in Accident & Emergency and knew how to cope with medical emergencies. But this? He had no training for this.

He was proud to see his friends all quiet and composed, the guys stoic and serious, the girls white-faced but in control as they fumbled with their oxygen masks. Everything was going to be all right, he told himself as he put his own on. This couldn't be it—the end. Only this morning, hours earlier, he'd awoken naked in bed with Roberta. Now, he couldn't see why he'd been so upset about it. He should have laughed it off, kissed her, told her he was sorry, told her the truth. Suddenly, secrets and promises held no attraction; reputation and status were empty words, hollow compared to the delight of waking next to the woman he'd wanted since the moment he'd first seen her.

He'd not been in Kerikeri long, but he'd built a life for himself there, had made good friends, and had grown to love all the members of the Goldsmith family. He couldn't believe they were nearly all here on the plane together. If they went down… if they were all lost… For a moment he half-wished Dominic was on board—maybe then the Almighty would take an interest in their plight. Then he was glad Dominic was miles away with his wife, and that Dominic's daughter, Emily, was at home with her grandmother, Noelle. They'd have each other to comfort them in their hour of need…

His thoughts were spiraling along with the plane. It was nothing like having his life flash before his eyes, but he couldn't seem to keep his thoughts straight. He had his phone in his pocket; he should text his mother, or Katrina, but he couldn't think what he could possibly say to them in one or two sentences that would express how he felt.

At that moment, Roberta's hand crept into his. He turned to look at her and saw her green eyes glistening.

"I'm sorry," she said, her voice muffled, hard to hear above the cries emanating from passengers behind him as they obviously saw the ground approaching.

"Don't be." He squeezed her fingers. "You know I'm crazy about you, right?"

He wasn't sure if she'd heard him. "I don't want to die," she said.

"We're not going to." He yanked up his oxygen mask, leaned across as she lifted hers, and kissed her, brief, hard. He had a flash of her eyes, brilliant green, sunlight on a dark river. Then he pushed her head so her forehead touched the seat in front and made sure Bianca had done the same. He reached across and gripped Elliot's hand in a silent gesture of commiseration.

Then he leaned down and assumed the crash position.

Chapter Five

Roberta's heart was racing so fast she could barely breathe. Children were crying, women were sobbing, and behind her she could hear someone, probably Mike, saying, "Oh fuck, oh fuck, oh fuck," his voice muffled through the oxygen mask.

Beside her, Bianca was quiet but shaking violently, and Roberta reached out a hand and gripped her sister's. It all felt like a dream. She knew the chances of being in a plane crash were rare—it was the safest form of transport, much safer than driving a car. What was the likelihood of survival? She risked a glance out of the window and saw that they had reached Rarotonga, and the ground was approaching at an alarming rate. They were going to hit bush and earth, not water. Was that better or worse?

She couldn't believe this was happening. There was no time, no time. She wanted to yell out to Phoebe that she loved her—poor Phoebe, who'd recovered from amnesia after an accident only to have to go through this. She wanted to tell all her friends how wonderful they were and that she loved them all, but everyone had hunkered down, and the sound was deafening, the plane juddering now as it descended rapidly.

She heard the squeaking, clunking noise as the wheels dropped and almost laughed at the thought of needing wheels when they were going to land in the treetops. The giggle rose inside her and burst out, and she saw Bianca turn to look at her and stifled the laughter, only to immediately have tears prick her eyes.

Oh Jesus. She was going to die today. She was really going to die. She'd never get married, grow old with her husband, never have children. Never sit up in the dark hours nursing them, never be a soccer mum or listen to them trying to learn the violin or comfort them when they'd broken up with their best friend. All the things she'd told herself she didn't need, didn't care about—suddenly, she wanted them more than anything, with a fierce longing that made her heart clench and her stomach twist.

And oh God, why hadn't she told Angus how she really felt about him? Why did everyone play these games of tiptoeing around each other, too afraid to say what was in their hearts in case they looked stupid or embarrassed themselves? He'd kissed her, hot and hard, and she'd seen regret in his eyes. He did have feelings for her, of course he did, or last night wouldn't have happened. Because it didn't matter how drunk she was, she knew she would never have ended up in bed with Rafe or Mike or any other guy she didn't have feelings for. They'd gone to bed together because there was an attraction there, and it was stupid to fight it.

They were married. The realization hit her, brought tears to her eyes. It meant nothing… it was foolish to think it… But the act of saying their vows, albeit drunkenly, the words stuttered and unremembered, had altered their relationship, changed something invisible in the links that bound them together. They would never be the same, not even when they got an annulment or a divorce. It wouldn't change the fact that, for a brief moment, he was her husband. She was his wife.

If they survived this, she was going to tell him how she felt. Put all her cards on the table. Not just that—she was going to tell everyone how she felt all the time and screw embarrassment and propriety. She'd never been particularly reticent anyway, but she was definitely going to change.

If they survived…

The plane lurched, and branches and leaves whipped at the undercarriage as the plane skimmed the tops of the trees. Behind her, someone vomited, while others prayed and cried. Her eyes were wet, her breaths coming fast. She closed her eyes, concentrating on the feel of Angus beside her, solid, reassuring. The plane hadn't nose-dived, and they weren't going to drown. The emergency services would be there soon. If they could just get to the ground…

At that moment, the world came to an end. There was a massive, deafening crunch. The plane met the ground with enough force to expel the breath from her lungs. She banged her forehead on the seat in front, hard enough to hurt her neck. The plane buckled as if it was made of paper, and around her the seats lurched, everything bending, twisting. People screamed, sobbed. One moment Bianca was beside her, and then she wasn't, torn away as green leaves replaced the cream interior. Angus's hand clamped on her thigh, fingers gripping so tight it hurt, and she clung to him as they tipped, spun, the sound of tearing metal echoing someone's scream.

It seemed to go on forever, although it must have only been twenty seconds or so, but it was like being on the worst rollercoaster ride ever, for a moment being weightless, then having the breath knocked out of her as she met the ground again, then feeling herself flung to the side or, at one moment she was sure, completely upside down. Her head throbbed, all her limbs hurt, and she squealed at the sensation of something sharp dragging down her arm, the skin burning as it tore.

And then, all of sudden, everything went still.

For a moment, she didn't move. She was turned in her seat toward Angus, her knees drawn up, and the seat in front of her wasn't where it should be, but was pressed almost up against hers. There was blood on her arm, which frightened her, but she could move it, and although she hurt all over, she had two arms, two legs, and her head was still attached to her body.

She'd survived. She was alive!

Oh Jesus, oh Jesus. She pushed herself up, unable to take in the bizarreness of the scene. It was like a post-apocalyptic game she'd played with Elliot once on the PlayStation, where the jungle had encroached on a city, creeping over buildings and cars. The right wall of the plane had been peeled away like a banana skin, and instead thick green leaves hung over the torn ceiling like a curtain, the sun slanting through them, throwing dappled light over the scene. Bianca's seat had gone completely.

Holy shit.

"Roberta?" On her left, Angus was fumbling at his seat belt. After releasing it, he turned in his seat to face her. "Fuck. You're bleeding."

"I'm okay." She felt him lift her arm and inspect it. "It's not bad, it was just a branch, it scratched it all the way down. I'm okay."

He cupped her face, lifted it to look into her eyes. He had a cut on his temple and blood on his cheek, but his blue eyes were clear. "Oh thank God," he said, pulling her into his arms.

She clung to him for a moment, just thankful to be alive, tears running down her face. "Oh, Angus."

He moved back and kissed her cheeks, her nose, her mouth, then hugged her again. "I'm so sorry," he said.

She didn't know what he was sorry for but clutched at his shirt and buried her face in his neck. "I thought we were going to die."

"I know."

"Oh Angus… Bianca!" She fought to unbuckle herself. Angus glanced past her and cursed under his breath, then looked around. She followed his gaze as her belt came undone. To their left, Elliot was already out of his belt, fighting to release Karen, who was sobbing in her seat. Further along, she could see Rafe and Phoebe, both moving. Oh God, thank you, thank you.

Then she twisted in her seat to look behind her. Her jaw dropped. The whole right side of the plane had been peeled back like a sardine can. Bianca, and Libby who'd been sitting behind her, had both gone. Mike still sat in the middle seat, hanging out into the bush, held there by his belt. He wasn't moving.

She turned back in her seat, watched Angus push himself up and envelop Elliot in a bear hug. "Fucking hell," Elliot said. "Holy fucking hell."

"How long before the emergency services get here, do you think?" Angus asked him.

"No idea how far we are from the airport. Could be ten minutes, could be an hour." Elliot had released Karen, and was now leaning across her, trying to help Rafe undo his seat belt. Rafe's seat had twisted, trapping the belt, and Roberta heard him swearing as he fought to get the thing undone. On his left, she saw Phoebe release herself and get to her feet, and their eyes met across the seating.

"You all right?" Roberta mouthed.

Phoebe nodded, although tears streamed down her face. "You?"

Roberta gave her a thumbs up, then glanced over her shoulder at the open plane and back to Phoebe, who put her hand over her mouth.

"We need to triage," Angus said, drawing her attention back to him.

"What?"

"It could be a while before the emergency services arrive," he said. "I'm a doctor—I have to help. We need to go through the plane, work out who's badly injured."

Rafe pushed himself up and leaned over the seat in front to help the woman there who was panicking, trying to get her belt undone. "What the fuck happened to the right side of the plane?"

"It's been torn away," Angus said.

"I want to find Bianca." Roberta felt sick. "I need to find her, and Libby."

Angus looked behind them, then moved around the seats. He helped out the woman sitting next to Mike, and then he and Elliot pulled their friend up by the seatbelt. Roberta clapped a hand over her mouth. Mike's midriff was covered in blood, his face white. His eyes were open, but unseeing.

Angus bent and looked at Mike's face, then felt for a pulse. His eyes met Elliot's and he shook his head.

Elliot ran his hands through his hair, then picked up a discarded blanket and laid it across their friend.

"Oh God." Roberta blew out a breath, shaking.

"Are you okay?" Angus took her face in his hands. "You have to keep it together. We're going to be needed now."

Roberta nodded, swallowing hard. She'd mourn Mike later. First, she had to see what had happened to her sister and Libby. She looked over the jagged edge of the plane. "There!" she said, seeing the right-hand strip of the plane not far away. "I'm going to find Bianca."

"I'll come with you," Angus said.

Elliot had paled at the thought of his sister being injured, but he nodded. "Rafe and I will assess the situation here."

"If someone's groaning, they're alive," Angus said. "Try to work out who needs attention. Put pressure on bleeding wounds. I'll be back as soon as we find the others."

Elliot nodded and started moving toward the front of the plane.

Roberta inched to the edge, Angus right behind her. In front of them was a large tree, and she leaned on it as she jumped down, falling forward onto her hands and knees. Angus landed beside her and pulled her up, and they pushed through the undergrowth toward the mangled part of the plane.

Her feet sank into the mulch and leaves of the forest floor, the rich smell rising to fill her nostrils. Bits of torn steel and debris from the plane littered the ground. To her shock, she saw a body in front of her, draped across a branch like a piece of clothing left to dry. It was a woman she didn't know, her gray hair matted with blood, her eyes open, staring up at the sky. Angus dropped to his haunches beside her and felt for a pulse. His gaze came up to meet Roberta's, and he gave a little shake of his head.

Her stomach clenched, and she turned and vomited into the bush. Holy shit, that had come from nowhere. She spat, took the crumpled serviette that Angus must have found in his pocket, and wiped her mouth.

"Sorry," she said, embarrassed, her eyes stinging. Mike was dead, and now this woman. What had happened to her sister?

"It's the body's natural reaction to shock, honey. It doesn't show lack of character." He stroked her back. "All right?" His eyes were brighter than the blue sky, and he held out his hand to her. She nodded and slid hers into it and let him lead her onward.

It wasn't far to the debris. A row of about eight seats formed a wall in the bush, several of them hanging from what was left of the plane. She could see instantly that the man at the front was dead, although Angus checked him anyway. Behind him, a woman sat on the ground, sobbing. Roberta bent to talk to her, but then heard someone call her name and her head whipped around to the seats behind.

"Bianca!" She rushed forward, emotion rushing through her at the sight of her sister apparently unharmed except for some scratches and bruises, and maybe a hurt arm considering the way she held it across her chest. "Oh, thank God." She stopped short at the look on Bianca's face, though, and her gaze fell on the woman still strapped into the seat behind her, hanging from the tree in which the piece of the plane had landed.

Libby's eyes were open, her face pale as milk. A long piece of metal had peeled off the side of the plane and now it protruded through her right thigh, which was covered in blood.

"Angus!" Roberta called, fear knifing through her.

He appeared at her side, gave Bianca a quick hug, then bent to look at their friend.

"Hey, Libby." He cupped her face, lifting her chin to look into her eyes. "How are you doing?"

"Hurts," she whispered.

"Okay, honey. I'm going to take a look, all right?"

Roberta moved back a little, watching with a thumping heart as Angus inspected the point where the metal pierced her friend, felt around the wound, tested Libby's reflexes, took her pulse. He worked deftly, unafraid of the blood and the little cries that Libby gave when he prodded the skin, and Roberta felt a surge of admiration for him.

She hadn't seen him in action before as a doctor, and she'd forgotten that he must have done a rotation in the A&E and in surgery.

"All right," he said. "I'm going to quickly check the other passengers here, see if I can find a first aid kit on the plane, and then I'll be back."

"Should we try to get the metal out?" Bianca asked him.

He shook his head. "She'll bleed out. I'm hoping the emergency services won't be long. Can you stay with her?"

Bianca nodded.

"Keep her calm, keep talking to her, reassure her. Don't let her move. We'll be back in a minute. Rob, come with me. You'll have to be my nurse." He flashed her a smile, and then he was off, moving toward the other passengers who were attempting to extricate themselves from the wreckage.

Roberta threw an arm around her sister and gave her a fierce hug. "I'm so glad you're okay."

"How are the others?"

"All right. A few bumps and bruises, nothing serious."

"Is Mike all right?" Libby whispered.

Roberta met Bianca's gaze. Bianca read the truth there and bit her lip, drawing in a shaky breath.

"Don't worry about anything now," Roberta said to Libby in as soothing voice as she could muster. "We'll be back as soon as we can."

She gave her sister a final hug.

"Roberta," Angus called, his voice firm.

"Coming!" She released her sister, gave her a quick smile, and moved on.

She'd never thought of herself as a nurse before. She wasn't sure she had the stomach for it, but she wasn't going to let Angus down. If she could help, she wasn't going to sit in a corner and cry. Not yet, anyway.

Chapter Six

They checked the other passengers on the torn piece of the plane, then returned to the main section, climbing up awkwardly. Roberta's heart rate was beginning to slow as her fear of imminent death died away, but it sped up again at the sound of cries and moans from the wounded passengers.

"The captain's dead," Elliot said, holding out a hand to pull them up. "The co-pilot's breathing but unconscious. I've made him comfortable, but I don't think there's much we can do for him at the moment."

"There are a few broken limbs in the front part of the plane," Rafe announced to Angus, coming over. "A couple you should have a look at."

"Can you check the child first?" Phoebe called out. They turned to see her cradling a toddler, maybe eighteen months old. The boy's eyes were open, but he wasn't crying. His mother lay unmoving, her eyes closed. Her husband's face was covered in tears as he smoothed hair off her forehead.

Angus moved to check the mother and felt for a pulse in her neck. "She's alive," he announced, and the husband gave a loud sob. Angus inspected a wound on the back of her head. "The ambulance will be here soon," he said to her husband. He took the blanket from the seat, folded it, and pressed it to the back of her head. "Hold this here, and keep talking to her," he instructed the man, showing him how. Then he turned to the child in Phoebe's arms. "What's his name?" he asked the father.

"Max. Is he…" The man couldn't finish the sentence.

Angus moved his hands quickly over the child, feeling his limbs, his torso. Phoebe helped him turn the boy over, and he checked his head, his back, before turning him around again. "Hi Max! Are you hurt anywhere?" The boy shook his head slowly, his gaze sliding to his mother. "He's fine," Angus said, "just a bit shaken up. Your mum has had a bump on the head, but the ambulance man will be here soon, okay? You stay here with your dad, and Phoebe will look after you." Phoebe nodded, relief on her face at the knowledge that the child was going to be all right. Angus straightened and took Roberta's hand. "Come on."

She followed him forward to where one of the flight attendants was attempting to comfort an elderly man with breathing problems.

"I'm a doctor," Angus said. "Where are the first aid kits?"

"Up there." She pointed to one of the lockers above the toilets. Her face was pale, scratched and bruised, but she looked composed and relieved to see a doctor on the plane.

Together, Angus and Roberta retrieved the first aid packs and examined the contents. There were sterile pads and bandages, bottles of tablets and vials of liquids, facemasks and gloves, and lots of equipment that Roberta had no idea about. Angus muttered as he read the labels on the medicines, then packed up the kit.

"Okay," he said. "We're going out to the debris to the south to see to a couple of badly injured passengers there, and then we'll come back, okay?"

The flight attendant nodded.

"You're doing a great job," he told her. "Keep everyone calm and reassure them the emergency services will be here soon. I'll only be a few minutes."

She swallowed hard and nodded.

Roberta pulled the strap of the pack over her head, followed him back through the plane, and jumped down into the bush again. "What can you do for Libby?" she asked as they pushed through the thick foliage. It was hot and humid, and she felt sweat pop onto her skin and soak her top.

"Not much," Angus replied. "There aren't a whole lot of pain-killing meds in this pack; it's mostly used for emergencies on the plane when you're in the air, like heart attacks or allergic reactions. We can't afford to move her as she'll start bleeding the moment we remove the piece of metal. It's awfully near her femoral artery, and if that gets cut, she's in real trouble." He pushed a branch out of the way and held it back for her. "We'll give her something for the pain, and we need to bind the wound of the guy behind her. Then we'll come back here and see to the breaks."

"Okay." She followed him to Libby, Bianca kneeling by her side, stroking her hair and talking to her softly. Angus opened one of the disinfectant wipes and cleaned his hands free of mud and blood, then snapped on a pair of gloves and made Roberta do the same.

"All right, Libby," he said, "I'm going to inject you with something to take away the pain, okay?"

She nodded. He took out one of the syringes, inserted it into one of the tiny bottles, and injected Libby. Almost immediately, she relaxed back in the seat, her pain-etched features softening.

"Is she going to be okay?" Bianca asked.

"The emergency services will be on their way soon," he said. Roberta noticed that he didn't answer her sister.

"I'll stay with her," Bianca told them.

"Are you okay?" Roberta asked her. "You're not hurt?" She was conscious of Bianca still holding her arm in an awkward way.

But Bianca just said, "Nothing that a couple of Panadol won't cure later," so Roberta nodded and followed Angus, who was already moving on to the next passenger. When they'd bound up the wound of the guy behind Libby, they started walking back to the plane.

"How bad is it, with Libby?" Roberta asked him.

He looked down at her, and she half-expected him to tell her everything was going to be all right, to give her platitudes. Instead, though, he said, "I don't know how long it's going to take the ambulances to get here. We're in the middle of the bush, and I've no idea how far we are from the road. It could be a while. It's a bad wound she's got, and she's already lost a lot of blood. But she's still lucid, which is a good sign. If Bianca can keep her still and stop her cutting that femoral artery, she stands a chance."

Roberta bit her lip and concentrated on climbing back into the plane. How could he remain so calm? She would never have made a good nurse. Even now, as she pulled herself up, she could hear cries of pain and fear, and she had to grit her teeth hard to stop herself shaking. They didn't have enough medication to help everyone. What was Angus going to do?

Luckily, she didn't have time to think about things as he led her through the plane, assessing the wounded, then starting to help those who needed them the most. She handed him wipes, pads, and bandages, helped him clean wounds and bind them, and occasionally aided him in dealing with breaks and other more serious injuries. She'd never have thought she would be able to stomach so much blood, but she was determined not to let him down.

Her admiration for him grew with every person he treated. He was so calm, so competent, and she watched the passengers react to his gentle manner, their panic dying down when he told them he was a doctor and that he'd do what he could for them.

"I wish I could do more," she said as they climbed over a twisted piece of the plane to reach the seats beyond it.

"Being a doctor isn't all about knowing what medicines to give," he told her. "Keeping people calm is a major part of the job, and you have a real talent for that." He didn't say any more, already turning to another wounded passenger, but Roberta felt a glow inside that didn't go away as she bent to help him.

She lost all track of time as they moved through the plane. How long had it been? Twenty minutes? Thirty? At one point they stopped when Phoebe brought them a drink and a chocolate bar, and then they were off again, Rafe and Elliot sometimes moving with them, shifting debris so they could get to the injured beneath it.

"I wonder if we've made the news yet," Phoebe said at one point, holding out a rubbish bag for Roberta to deposit bloodied pieces of tissue.

"Oh God, Mum." Roberta went cold at the thought of their mother discovering what had happened via the TV. "We should call her."

"I've tried. No signal."

"She's going to be worried sick."

"I know."

"And Libby's mum, too," Roberta realized.

"How is she?" Phoebe wanted to know.

"Libby? Hanging on. Literally. She's still strapped in the seat, but Angus said we shouldn't let her out because then we'll have to remove the piece of metal from her leg, and it's likely she'll bleed out."

"Oh no." Phoebe paled.

"Bianca's with her."

"I can't believe she's okay after what happened to the plane."

"I think she's hurt her arm," Roberta said, "but considering how the whole side of the plane was ripped off, I think she's come out of it relatively well."

"Poor Mike," Phoebe whispered, tears filling her eyes.

"I know. It's so awful. I didn't tell Libby—I didn't want her to get upset while she had that metal in her leg. But she'll have to be told."

"We could all have died," Phoebe said. "We've been so lucky."

"It doesn't feel very lucky at the moment." But Roberta knew her sister was right. How often did people survive a plane crash like this?

"Wait," Phoebe said, placing a hand on her sister's arm. "Can you hear that?"

The two girls listened, straining their ears, and then Roberta heard it, way off in the distance—sirens.

"Oh, thank Christ." She almost cried with relief.

"Come on," Angus said, moving to the next passenger. "It could take them a while to get here. We can't stop now."

"Slave driver," Roberta grumbled, but she followed him anyway.

In actual fact, it was about another twenty minutes before the first emergency services personnel appeared, pushing through the bush carrying medical bags, stretchers, and other equipment.

Angus, Roberta, Elliot, Rafe, and some of the others who'd been helping explained the situation, pointing out the more serious injuries, and gradually the paramedics and firefighters began moving through the plane, assessing the damage and dealing with the injured people.

"I want to help Libby," Roberta told one of the paramedics as they tried to tend to her, pushing them away.

"You're injured, ma'am," the paramedic said, "and you need attention. Your friend will be helped, and you'll be able to visit her at the hospital." He pushed her gently onto a stretcher, and Roberta, suddenly exhausted, lay back and let them carry her through the undergrowth.

Why was she so tired? Her whole body ached, and her arm throbbed, the skin crusty with dried blood. Where was Angus? And her sisters? What was going to happen to Libby?

And Mike… poor Mike… tears leaked through her eyes at the thought of the friend she'd lost. She'd never been that close to him; he'd been a strange guy, oddly difficult to like, and she'd never quite known what Libby had seen in him, but he'd been Libby's partner and one of their close-knit group, and the thought of him not being there anymore shocked her to the core.

Everything was changing… nothing would ever be the same. She'd thought that Phoebe's accident had been bad, but how would they recover from this?

Chapter Seven

Angus spent some time with the paramedics, explaining what treatment he'd given to the more seriously injured passengers. He and Elliot refused to leave until the firefighters had cut Libby from the wreckage, and Elliot held her hand while they carried her on a stretcher toward the flashing lights where the ambulances were waiting. Only then did they give in to their gentle pressure, and Angus let someone bathe the wound on his head before climbing into the ambulance and letting them take him to the hospital.

Man, he was tired. He hadn't realized how bruised he was—his body felt as if it had been through an old-fashioned mangle. He felt terribly sore down his left hip, and when he mentioned it to the paramedic travelling in the ambulance with him and two other passengers, the paramedic took a quick look and showed him the large contusion spreading across the skin, which was already starting to turn a vivid shade of purple. It must have happened when the plane first landed with that God-awful crash. All the breath had left his body with a whoosh, and his body had slammed against the seat, which had twisted, the metal bending as easily as if it were made out of plasticine. That would take a while to heal.

Oh well, he'd come out of it a lot better than many others. As he'd walked away from the plane, he'd taken a last look back and had been shocked at the sight of the loose wires and bent metal, the debris scattered over a huge radius. It could have been so much worse. The pilot had done an amazing job getting them to the ground without losing more lives. Emotion rose in him at the thought of those who had died, including the pilot himself, and Mike.

What a shitty day it had been, starting with the discovery of the mess he'd made of the situation with Roberta. He wished he could rewind time and go back to the previous evening, when everything had been all right. He'd have refused that final drink with her, would have gone to bed alone and avoided that catastrophe.

Like most men, Angus didn't cry easily, but tears pricked his eyes, whether at the loss of his friend or at his own idiocy, he wasn't sure. The doctor part of him knew it was shock, but knowing it didn't stop the tears running down his cheeks, or his hands from shaking.

"It's all right," the paramedic soothed, placing a blanket around his shoulders. She was young and Polynesian, her long brown hair wound in a tight bun, her chocolate-colored eyes filled with sympathy.

"Sorry," he said, wiping his face. "I lost a friend back there. I think the shock's setting in."

"Of course. You've been through an incredible ordeal. Don't worry, we'll get you to the hospital and check you over, and then you can have a nice cup of tea or coffee and something to eat. You'll feel better then."

He'd done this himself, and recognized her low, comforting tone, her gentle touch as she rubbed his upper arm, establishing human contact. He'd experienced shock before, when Jamie died, but it hadn't been like this. That had been almost too deep to process, a complete confusion at the thought that he'd never be able to talk to his brother again. The grief had been like an insidious disease, eating into his flesh and bones and creeping over him so gradually it wasn't until much later that he'd finally realized the extent of his loss.

This wasn't the same—this was like being hit around the head with a baseball bat. His plane had tumbled from the sky to the ground. But he was still alive. He'd survived a plane crash. Holy shit. The enormity of it made his head hurt.

He wondered how the others were doing. He'd seen them take the girls, Phoebe and Bianca, and the guys soon after, Rafe and Elliot protesting all the way as they were encouraged to leave. Roberta had stayed with him for a while until she, nearly dropping with exhaustion, had been persuaded to go. Where was she now, already at the hospital?

Everyone reacted to shock differently, and in the past he'd seen some people collapse with grief, sobbing uncontrollably, while others sat staring into space and couldn't be moved.

But Roberta had been amazing at the crash site, sticking to his side and not flinching once as he asked her to help him bind the wounds, even when a patient cried out in pain and there was blood everywhere.

He should have guessed she'd be great. She was so down-to-earth and practical; he loved that about her.

He lay back and closed his eyes, his mind filling with the vision of green leaves overhead, and the sound of screeching metal. He brushed it from his mind and pictured Roberta instead, the way she'd looked that morning, lying in bed. Soft tanned skin, rumpled hair, sleepy surprise on her face, her green eyes wide as she stared at him. He'd wanted to kiss her so badly, to lie back and pull her on top of him and make love to her. Maybe he should have. After what had just happened, he wished he had.

As the ambulance sped along the road, he found himself wondering why she was still single. She was young, not yet thirty, and although not pretty and dainty the way her twin sisters were, she was strikingly beautiful, and full of spirit. She'd be a catch for any sensible guy. About six months ago she'd dated someone for a while, but then he'd disappeared from the scene and he hadn't seen her with anyone else since. He vaguely remembered in the early days Elliot saying something about her having dated someone at university who'd 'scarred her for life,' in his words, but Elliot had been unwilling to provide any other details. Maybe he should ask her. But then what was the point of that when he was trying so hard to keep his distance?

His thoughts drifted, spiraled, and it was only when the ambulance stopped and the engine died that he realized he'd dozed off, worn out with the physical and emotional exertion of the day.

Following the paramedic's directions, he entered the hospital. Based in the capital city of Avarua, the small hospital boasted eighty beds and two theatres. It was heaving now, with people lying on beds in the corridors and others sitting on the rows of chairs, sipping from hot drinks as they answered questions from the staff.

He waved away a query about his injuries; nothing could be done about his hip, and there were others who needed attention more than he did, and crossed the main floor of the hospital to where he could see Elliot on the far side, sitting with the others in a small group.

"Hey." Elliot stood as he approached, and they bear-hugged, and he did the same to Rafe before hugging the girls.

Bianca had her arm in a sling, "Sprained, not broken," she told him. They all bore scratches and bruises, and they all looked tired and emotionally drained, but at least they were alive.

"Where's Roberta?" he asked.

"Just having that gouge on her arm seen to," Phoebe said. "It was pretty deep and still bleeding. Here she is."

He turned to see her walking up to them. Her arm was bound in a bandage, and she looked tired and pale, but she smiled when she saw him. "Hey, you."

"Hey, Nurse Goldsmith." He smiled. "You did an amazing job today."

"Aw. I only did what you told me to do."

"No, I'm serious. I couldn't have done it without you." He was conscious that the others had turned away as if to try to give them some privacy. At that moment, he didn't really care what they thought. He opened his arms, and when Roberta walked into them, he wrapped them around her.

What would it feel like to be married to her? To know that she was his, loyal and faithful, there as support when he needed someone? In his bed every night, turning to him in the dark, her mouth searching for his?

She rested her cheek on his chest, and he pressed his lips to the top of her head.

"How's Libby?" she whispered.

"I don't know. I just got here."

"She's in surgery," Elliot said, his arm around Karen.

"Has anyone told her about Mike yet?" Angus asked.

Elliot shook his head. "She wasn't conscious when she went in. She'll have that news to wake up to."

Phoebe pressed her fingers to her mouth, and Rafe tightened his arm around her. Bianca curled up in her seat, resting her cheek on her knees, and closed her eyes.

"Poor Libby," Roberta said. "How awful."

"Have you contacted anyone back home?" Angus asked.

"Elliot rang Mum," Roberta said. "She'd heard about the crash and was out of her mind with worry. And so relieved to hear we're all okay. Most of us." She swallowed hard and turned her head, burying her face in his shirt. "I keep thinking about Mike. It's so horrible…"

"I know." He tightened his arms, wishing he could magic all the hurt away for her.

"I can't believe it was only this morning that we were in bed," she whispered, moving so that his back was to the others.

"I know. It seems crazy."

"I suppose you lost the certificate," she said in a small voice.

He nodded. "It was in my backpack. I guess we might get our stuff back eventually, but I'm not holding out any hope." Most of the overhead lockers had opened and the contents had been scattered over the crash site.

"It doesn't change the fact that we're married," she said.

He opened his mouth to answer her, but at that moment his mobile phone, which was the only thing he'd had in the back pocket of his jeans, started to ring.

"Sorry. Hold on." He pulled it out, and his heart leapt into his mouth at the sight of Katrina's name on the screen. "I need to take this, sorry."

Roberta nodded and dropped her arms. He turned and walked away, through the doors into the warm Rarotonga sunshine. "Hello?"

"It's me," Katrina said. She was crying, sobbing with relief, her Russian accent even more prominent with her heightened emotion. "Oh, Angus. I thought you were dead."

"No, I'm okay." He tipped his face up to the sun. "You saw the crash on TV?"

"It's been all over the news. I had your flight number, so I knew it was yours. I've been trying to get through to the airline—they gave out an emergency number, but I haven't been able to get through. Oh my God, I can't believe you're alive…"

He spoke to her softly for a while, reassuring her. In the background, little Katie started crying, and his stomach clenched.

"Is she okay?" he asked.

"She's just crying because I'm crying."

"You should go to her. I hate hearing her so upset."

"I will. I just… I thought I'd lost you. I couldn't bear it if I lost you, Angus."

"I'll always be here for you," he told her firmly, glad he hadn't gone into the details of the crash. "I'm not going anywhere."

"You'll come and visit us soon? It would be good to see you."

"I'll come down in two weeks. We'll go out to dinner, me, you, and Katie. Would you like that?"

"It would be lovely. I'm so glad you're alive, Angus."

"Me too," he said earnestly. "Take care of yourself and baby Katie."

"I will. Goodbye." She hung up.

Angus turned around, feeling tired. Roberta was sitting now, next to Bianca, her arms around her sister, but her gaze was on him, curious but too polite to ask. He wished he could tell her everything, but he'd made a promise, and he wouldn't break it for the world. Maybe one day, everything would become clear. But for now, for better or worse, he'd made his bed, and he had to lie in it.

Chapter Eight

Five days later

Roberta took a seat at the end of the line of chairs, behind Elliot and Karen. Elliot turned to look at her, and held out a hand to grasp hers.

"You okay?" he mouthed.

She nodded, even though she wasn't. Who could be okay on a day like this? Funerals were horrible even when the deceased was an elderly person, but the fact that it was someone her own age made her feel twisted inside.

She watched as, in the front row, Libby's brother, Alastair, pushed her in her wheelchair to a space they'd left for her beside Mike's mother, Petra. Fresh out of hospital, Libby's skin was the shade of milk, and she had not an ounce of color in her cheeks. Roberta couldn't imagine how it must feel to bury your partner before the age of thirty. Life could be so fucking cruel.

Roberta watched Karen lean her head on Elliot's shoulder, and his arm come up around her. Funerals were such lonely places. You're born alone, you die alone, she thought, and yet people clung to each other in that space in between as if they were on a life raft that could carry them to safety.

She looked out of the large windows at the rain beating down from the dull gray sky. July—the height of winter in the southern hemisphere—was turning out to be wet and miserable. It seemed apt; it would have been all wrong if the sun had been shining.

Someone sat next to her, and she turned her head to find Angus looking at her, his eyes full of concern. "How are you doing?" he murmured. She gave a little nod, a half-shrug. "You look tired," he said.

"I haven't been sleeping well." It was a massive understatement—she'd been sleeping terribly, if she'd slept at all. Vivid dreams of the crash kept jerking her awake, where she'd lie with a hammering heart, covered in sweat, tears streaming down her face.

"You need to take care of yourself," he told her. "Maybe see someone to talk over what happened. All of us are going to have PTSD to some extent, and it's nothing to laugh at."

"I'm not laughing."

"No." He looked sad.

Phoebe sat a few seats down with Rafe, the two of them with heads almost touching as they talked quietly. Roberta's mother, Noelle, sat with Dominic and Fliss, who'd flown back as soon as they'd heard about the crash. Little Emily was staying with a friend. Next to them sat Bianca with Libby's sister, Emilia. Emilia was crying, and Bianca's face was full of sorrow. The rest of the large room was filled with Mike's family and friends, many of them also police officers, people she'd never met, united by their grief.

Her gaze came back to Angus, and she took the opportunity to study him while he was looking away. He was such a handsome man, tall, broad-shouldered, his dark-gray suit fitting him perfectly. His crisp white shirt made his tanned skin look darker. Although his hair was cropped short, it too was dark—she wouldn't have been surprised if he had some Maori blood in him. Up close like this, she could see a chickenpox scar on his jaw, and four freckles on his cheekbone.

He glanced at her then, a small smile appearing on his lips. "What?"

"Those freckles on your cheekbone are in the shape of the Southern Cross."

"That's so I can always find my way home."

She smiled back, then remembered where they were, and her smile faded.

Angus obviously saw the emotion pass across her face. "Aw," he said. "I miss him too."

"I didn't know him that well," she said. "He wasn't a close friend, even though I saw him quite a bit with Libby. I don't know why I'm so upset."

"Strictly speaking, grief isn't about the person who's died—it's about us, and what's happening in our lives. Why do you think so many people got upset when Princess Diana died? They didn't know her personally, but they felt for her family, for her young boys, and she represented the end of the kind of romantic lifestyle that lots of people dream about. Mike was the same age as you, so his passing is going to make you reassess your life and think about your own mortality. And you love Libby, so of course it's going to be upsetting."

That was part of it, of course, but she still didn't know why she felt quite so bad. If she was honest, she hadn't even liked Mike that much. He'd been arrogant and overbearing, and his lack of a sense of humor had meant that she had never really connected with him. Elliot had been the same; he'd put up with the guy because they worked together, but she had the feeling that her brother had been annoyed when Mike had first struck up a relationship with Libby two years ago, maybe feeling that she deserved better. Mike and Libby had been such an odd couple; Libby was carefree and bubbly and such fun to be with, and some of her shine had vanished when she was with Mike. They'd never been a loving sort of couple, never the sort to be caught holding hands or kissing.

How terrible to be thinking these thoughts at his funeral. She was such an awful person. She should be remembering all the wonderful things he'd said and done… except she couldn't think of any. She could only think of Libby with that horrific piece of metal spearing her thigh, and the way the air had been jolted out of her body when they'd crashed, and the screams that just wouldn't go away…

Angus's arm came around her, and she realized tears were streaming down her face.

"I'm sorry," she whispered, but he just took the square out of the top pocket of his jacket and handed it to her, and kept his arm tight around her as the priest walked out to start the service.

Roberta tried to tell herself that she shouldn't rely on Angus to comfort her—he wasn't her boyfriend, and they weren't really married, plus she'd promised not to draw attention to what had happened in Las Vegas. But then he gave a long sigh, and she thought that maybe he needed comforting too. He was right, it didn't really matter how close they'd been to Mike. He was a friend of theirs, and they were all dealing with the after-effects of the crash and the loss of a member of their circle. Of course they were all going to feel it deeply.

So she rested her head on his shoulder, and let his gentle stroking on her arm soothe her as the priest talked about Mike, trying to capture a whole lifetime and do it justice in the short space of time available to him.

Afterward, they filed outside, standing in small groups beneath the sheltered walkway and talking quietly while the rain poured down on the grass. Roberta watched her mother walk arm-in-arm with Mike's mother, Petra, examining the flowers that people had sent. The two women had been friends for a long time, finding solace in each other when their husbands passed away within a year of each other. Petra was warm and gentle, and she didn't deserve to lose her eldest son, too. But then who did deserve to lose a loved one? There was no justice in the world, Roberta thought, feeling hollow inside. Life was so cruel.

"Are you coming back to the house?" Elliot asked them all. Petra and her family had laid on sandwiches and drinks for everyone.

"We'll come," Phoebe said, gesturing to Rafe. "We'll take you, Bianca, if you want." She looked at Roberta. "Do you want to come with us?"

Roberta had travelled with them to the crematorium, so she didn't have her car. But suddenly, the thought of going back to the house was the absolute last thing she wanted to do.

Elliot frowned. "Are you okay?"

"I…" A tear ran down her face, and she brushed it aside hastily, only to have more join it. "I'm sorry," she said, dissolving into tears. "I don't know what's wrong with me."

"Hey, come on." Angus pulled her into his arms and hugged her. "I think I might take her home," he told Elliot. "She said she's not sleeping well, so I might give her a sleeping pill and put her to bed."

Roberta was too upset to worry about what they thought of that. "Tell Libby I'm sorry," she whispered, struggling to keep in control. Her sisters hugged her, and then she let Angus lead her away to his car.

He opened the door for her, and she slid into the seat. He leaned across her and clipped in her seatbelt, the smell of his aftershave filling her nostrils as he brushed against her. Then he closed the door and went around and got in the driver's side, started the car, and set off toward Waimate North.

"I'm sorry," she said softly, trying to staunch the flow of tears as he drove. "I don't know what's wrong with me."

"Stop apologizing," he scolded, glancing over at her. "You've been through a terrible trauma. It's only to be expected."

But Phoebe had been in the same crash, and Bianca. They'd known Mike the same way she had. They hadn't been bawling their eyes out at the funeral.

His passing is going to make you reassess your life and think about your own mortality, Angus had said. That's what it was. Since the crash, all she could think about was the fact that she was nearly thirty, still single, and with no foreseeable chance of having a family and settling down. Would anyone even notice if she died?

Of *course* they would; sensible Roberta knew her family and friends would be devastated. But at that moment, she felt as if it might have been better if she'd died in the crash instead of Mike. Angus wasn't interested in her and couldn't wait to erase their stupid evening from his mind. Ian hadn't wanted her. She'd never gotten over him, not really; she could tell herself she had every minute of every day, but it wasn't true.

With a start, she realized Angus was turning onto her drive, heading toward the house. They'd gone the whole way without talking, with her lost in her own world.

He pulled up and turned off the engine, got out, and ran around to open her door, turning his collar up against the rain. "Come on," he said, offering her his hand. She let him pull her up and, without releasing her, he led her to the front door. She tried to put the key in but fumbled and it slipped from her grasp. Angus picked it up and unlocked the door, then led the way in.

It wasn't late, only four thirty, but the light was already starting to fade from the gray sky. "Come with me," he said, leading her through to the kitchen.

He'd been to the house several times when she'd had everyone around for drinks in the summer, and so he knew where she kept her liquor. He took out a bottle of brandy and poured a generous amount into a glass while she stood leaning against the kitchen counter, shaking. He watched her drink it all, not smiling even when she shuddered, and then he led her down the corridor to her bedroom.

"You need to go to bed," he said firmly, pulling back the duvet.

Roberta stood in the doorway, her arms folded tightly across her chest. She didn't want to go to sleep. If she went to sleep, she'd dream, and then she'd wake up in the middle of the night frightened and alone, and it would only make things ten times worse.

"Roberta," he said, taking a step toward her. "God, please, you're breaking my heart…"

She covered her face with her hands and burst into tears.

"Oh Jesus, come here, you poor girl." He put an arm around her shoulders and, before she knew it, had lifted her up into his arms. He carried her over to the bed and climbed on with her, turned so his back was against the pillows with her on his lap, and then leaned back.

"I'm sorry," she said through her sobs, but she couldn't have stopped even if he'd wanted her to.

All he said, though, was, "Let it all out, honey. There's only me here. Just let it go."

So she did, not bothering to hold back. She cried until her face and hands and his shirt were wet, and she was all stuffed up, and all Angus did was stroke her back and hand her tissues, and murmur in the growing darkness about how everything was going to be all right.

Chapter Nine

Angus held Roberta for a long, long time, while the rain beat on the windows and the world gradually turned dark. At one point, one of her cats came into the room and jumped onto her washing bin, and from there onto the bedside table and then onto the bed. It curled up behind her knees, and Roberta sighed, so he knew she was still awake.

She'd cried for a while, but even when her tears finally stopped she still didn't move, and Angus was content to lie there and stroke her back, just enjoying the feel of her in his arms.

At least she was quiet now, her emotion spent. She'd wept all through the service, silent tears that had trickled down her cheeks despite her attempts to wipe them away, and when he'd taken her home she'd looked so forlorn that he'd been unable to resist comforting her, even though he'd known he should have just put her to bed and then left the house.

He liked the fact that she wasn't doll-like—she was at least five-nine, with long toned limbs; she didn't feel as if she would break if he squeezed her too tight. But she felt soft, her skin smooth beneath his fingers, her breasts pressing against his ribs like small pillows. Her hair, slightly damp from the rain, smelled of warm muffins from the baking she did every day in the café. She wore a black skirt and a pale pink, long-sleeved top that lent her a touch of girliness with a strip of pink lace around the neck.

This was a time out of time, a moment that would never come around again, and he was happy to take advantage of it and hold her while the tsunami of emotion washed over her. It would pass, it always did. She'd probably doze off, and then he'd extricate himself gently, cover her with the duvet, and head off.

How nice it would be, though, to stay. To take off his clothes, slip beneath the covers with her, and pull her against him. To make love to her, to feel her shapely body, to be inside her and give her pleasure. To watch her fall asleep and then drift off himself, knowing she'd be there when he awoke.

It was a wonderful fantasy, but it couldn't work. It was a crying shame, but there was nothing to be done about it.

She hadn't moved for a while. Had she dozed off? He lifted his head to try to look and she shifted in his arms, moving away a little so she could look up at him.

"Hey," he said, smiling. "How are you feeling?"

"Better." She removed the clip holding her hair back and ran her hands through the brown locks. "I must look terrible."

"You look lovely, as always." He meant it. Her eyes were red and her face a bit blotchy, but she still took his breath away.

"Do you have to go?" Her gaze rose to meet his, her green eyes bright.

He should say yes. Take the opportunity to escape before he did anything stupid.

"Not if you don't want me to," his mouth said of its own accord.

Her lips curved up a little, and she lowered down onto her side, propping her head on her hand. Facing her, Angus mirrored her pose, stretching out his legs and avoiding the cat that now curled up between them.

"Jasmine's wondering what the hell's going on," she said, scratching the cat between its ears. "She's not used to having a man around the house."

"What about that guy you dated six months ago? What happened to him?"

"Coby? That was never serious."

"He seemed pretty keen on you."

Her lips curved up. "Are you jealous?" He was, he realized, but he just raised an eyebrow, and she chuckled, dropping her arm to rest her head on the pillow. "We both knew it wasn't going anywhere," she said. "I was lonely, that's all."

"I don't understand why you're still single," he said.

"I'm not," she replied, amused, and he realized she was talking about the service they'd had in Vegas.

"You know what I mean," he told her wryly. "You're gorgeous, funny, warm, sexy. I thought men would be falling over themselves to ask you out."

"I could say the same about you."

He smiled. "Touché."

"It's about the signals we give out, isn't it? I don't go out much, and when I do, I'm with friends. I keep to myself. I haven't been looking for a mate, and I think men pick up on that."

"Why haven't you been looking?" He was curious. Was this about the man Elliot had referred to?

She sucked her bottom lip, her gaze sliding past him, to the rainy night. "Something happened a few years ago. I got badly burned. I thought I'd got over it, but I haven't, not really. I think all this," and she gestured at her face, implying her recent emotion, "is connected in some way."

"What happened?" he asked softly.

She took a breath and blew it out. "Late in my second year at university, I met a guy. He was a chef, and the owner of a chain of restaurants, based in Christchurch, but he'd come as a visiting speaker. He was a bit older than me, but I liked him immediately. We got talking after the lecture, and he asked me out to dinner. We went to one of his restaurants, so we had the best table, amazing service, the most expensive food. I had stars in my eyes, and when he asked to see me again, of course I said yes."

Angus wasn't sure where this was going yet. He already wanted to punch the guy's teeth down his throat, but he kept quiet and just nodded, waiting for the rest of the story.

"On the third date," she continued, "we went to bed together. I'd only had a couple of other partners and didn't know much about sex, and he… well, he had a few tricks up his sleeve. By the end of the evening, I was lost, and I think he knew it. It was then that he told me he was married."

Angus's eyebrows rose. "Married?"

"Yeah. I got angry, and he was apologetic and said he just hadn't been able to resist me. He said he'd never had an affair before, and I still believe that was true. We talked all night about what we were going to do. He said he'd married young and still cared for his wife, but that they led separate lives, and he was lonely. He said he'd fallen in love with me."

"What did you do?"

"He asked if he could continue to see me whenever he was in Auckland. He said he'd help me get an apartment so he could stay with me when he came up. And I said yes. Looking back, I suppose I was his mistress, but I didn't see it like that at the time. When we were together, we were a couple, and everyone treated us like one. It was good, for a long time. I liked having my freedom. I was able to see my friends in the week and then give him all my attention when he was there. It worked well for several years."

"Did he leave his wife?"

"No. And I didn't ask him to. I don't know why. I suppose I feared that he'd say no. When we were together, it was as if she didn't exist. He spent a lot of time with me, most weekends. I was happy the way things were."

"You weren't jealous?"

"I didn't let myself dwell on it. I was busy at uni, then I was learning the business, working all the hours God gave me in various restaurants and cafés. I didn't have time to think about it."

Angus knew this wasn't going to have a happy ending. "But…"

"But… After five years, one weekend he arrived at the apartment, sat me down, and told me his wife was pregnant."

Angus closed his eyes. "Jesus."

A touch of color appeared in her cheeks. "I suppose I'd fooled myself into thinking they didn't sleep together. Deep down, I hoped that one day he'd tell me he loved me more than her, and that he was going to leave her. But to find out he was having a family…" She bit her lip. "He tried to convince me that nothing was going to change, but of course I knew it would. I knew then that I'd been fooling myself. When he was at work the next day, I packed my bags and left."

"How long ago was this?"

"About… two years, I guess. I drove up here, to my parents. I hadn't told anyone about him, but I broke down and told them everything. They were horrified; they'd thought I was living on my own and happy in Auckland. I stayed with them for a while. Then my grandfather died—my mum's dad. He'd been a builder and had made a lot of money in Australia, and he left all the money to Mum. So they started up the Brides business, and gave us all some money of our own. I put mine down as a deposit on this house and set up the café."

"What about the guy—what was his name?"

She blew out a breath. "Ian."

"What about Ian? Have you seen him since?"

"He rang me a lot in the early days, trying to convince me to come back. I think he really loved me. That might sound ridiculous, but I think it's possible to have feelings for two people at once. It's been hard. When Dad died, Ian came up for the night. We didn't sleep together; he just held me while I cried. I haven't heard from him for about six months now, though. I miss him, but when it comes to it, he didn't want me enough to leave his wife. He had five years to do that, and he didn't."

"Did she have the baby?"

"Yes, a boy, and she's pregnant again now." Her eyes glistened. "I've spent the last two years trying to get over him, and I thought I had, but after the crash, and Mike, and what happened with us…" A tear spilled over her lashes. "I suppose it brought all the feelings back."

Angus felt that like a punch to his gut. "Oh, sweetheart."

"You don't have to feel sorry for me. I know I was stupid, with Ian. So fucking naive. But it hurts that he didn't want me. Not enough, anyway."

Angus couldn't help himself—he reached out and cupped her cheek, stroking it with his thumb. "I don't understand why. You're so beautiful. So full of life. He was crazy not to have chosen you."

A tear ran down her cheek. She dashed it away angrily. "I hate myself for being like this. I hate self-pity in other people. I don't want to feel like this."

"One day, you'll meet the right guy," he said helplessly. "You deserve so much more."

"I just want to be wanted. Is that so bad?"

"Of course not."

Her green eyes were full of pain. And he'd contributed to some of it by saying what they'd done was a terrible mistake.

"I want you," he said, knowing it was the wrong thing to say, but desperate to wipe the anguish from her expression.

"Don't." Her bottom lip trembled. "Don't lie to me, Angus. You're my friend."

"I'm not lying. I've wanted you since the first moment I met you at the bar with Elliot. It's just… it's complicated. I can't explain why, and that's not fair to you. You deserve so much more." He felt awful asking her to trust him when she'd placed her trust in another man and had been betrayed so badly.

Another tear traced a path down her cheek.

"Don't cry," he murmured. He slid his hand into her hair, running the silky strands through his fingers.

Turning her head, she closed her eyes and kissed his palm.

"You're so beautiful," he said. "I'm sorry he hurt you. I want to smash his face in for that."

Her lips curved up a tiny bit. "I thought you didn't like me."

He gave a short laugh. "I do. More than you could know."

"I know the marriage thing was a mistake," she whispered. "And I'm not expecting anything. But…" Her gaze dropped to his mouth. "Would you kiss me?"

Holy shit, it was absolutely the worst thing he could do at that moment. He needed to get up off the bed, shove on his shoes, and walk out into the stormy night.

"I shouldn't," he said, his voice husky. But of their own volition, his fingers were slipping through her hair to cup the back of her head.

"I know," she replied.

But they both knew he was going to.

He lowered his lips to hers, and her mouth was soft and cool. She parted her lips and he swept his tongue inside, and he grew hard at the slick, sweet taste of her, and her sigh that turned into a moan as he deepened the kiss.

He'd dreamed about this, fantasized about it, about holding her, kissing her, touching her. He had no excuse now—he wasn't drunk, and he knew he should be the gentleman and not take advantage of her when she was vulnerable and emotional.

But he wanted her—God, how he wanted her. And Roberta wanted him. Her arms came up around his neck, and she rolled into his embrace, brushing her knee up the outside of his thigh before hooking her leg over him to bring them closer together.

He was lost, and there was nothing he could do about it.

Chapter Ten

Roberta knew she was being dumb. Angus had already told her that their fake marriage was a mistake. It was clear that he desired her, but he'd practically told her he was hiding something from her, and that was the last thing she needed after the messy relationship she'd had with Ian. How did she get herself into these situations?

By reacting on instinct, she thought. She wished she wasn't like that, but she didn't know any other way to be. She'd always acted first, thought later. She longed to be like her sisters, quiet and cautious, weighing up the pros and cons of a situation before leaping in with both feet. But she wasn't. She was hot-headed and impulsive, too impatient to test the waters and wait and see.

Like now, for example. She should have told Angus thank you for bringing me home, then sent him away, made a cup of tea, and gone to bed with a good book.

She shouldn't be tugging his shirt free from his trousers, sliding her hand beneath the crisp white cotton, and scraping her nails across his warm skin. She shouldn't be thrusting her tongue into his mouth, adding her sighs to his groans, and pressing her breasts against his chest. And she definitely shouldn't be thinking about whether she had a condom in the drawer.

But fuck it, they were young, they were alive, and they wanted each other. They'd escaped death by a whisker. Did there need to be a better reason than that to enjoy physical pleasure with one another? Roberta didn't care about what had happened, or where this was leading, or the marriage certificate, or anything in fact except that she could feel his erection pressing against her lower belly, and it was long and hard and holy Jesus, she really wanted him inside her, right now.

She sank her other hand into his hair, hoping desperately that his principles weren't going to get the better of him. Knowing Angus, he was likely to try to persuade her that this was a mistake and that he should do the 'right thing' and leave, but she wanted him to take advantage of her. Did he know that?

And anyway, it was all legal. They were married. She stifled a giggle. It was fun to play at wedded bliss.

Then she felt his hand rest on the knee of the leg she'd wrapped around his hips. Was he going to push her away? His thumb slid on one side of her kneecap, his fingers on the other, and she tensed as he lifted his head a little to look down at her.

Please, please don't say you shouldn't.

"You're sure?" he murmured.

She nodded, so eagerly that he gave a short laugh, and then he was sliding his hand up from her knee, pushing up her skirt so he could feel her thigh. She was wearing thigh-highs, and when he got to the top of them, he brushed the tips of his fingers around the elastic, across her skin, and she shivered.

"I want you," he whispered. "I can't resist you. You're so fucking beautiful."

She caught her breath, his compliment taking her by surprise. "Even with panda eyes and a blotchy face?"

His lips curved up. "Even with." He cupped her face and stroked his thumb across her cheek. "I know this is crazy, but you've only had a shot of brandy, right?"

"Right."

"You know what you're doing."

"Totally."

"I don't want you to regret it."

"I won't. I swear. I just want to feel alive, Angus."

His brow furrowed. "I know."

"How can this be wrong? I want you." She brushed her lips against his. "I need you. I'm not expecting anything more. Just this once…"

He nodded, and then he crushed his lips to hers, plunging his tongue into her mouth, and she moaned and squirmed against him.

Sliding a hand behind her back, he unpopped the catch of her bra, and then his warm hands were travelling up to her breasts. Sighing, she closed her eyes as he pushed up her top and kissed down her neck, and at the feel of his hot mouth covering a nipple, she moaned and rocked her hips against his.

Wanting to see those defined muscles she'd glimpsed in Vegas, she unbuttoned his shirt, then stroked across his pecs. He kept himself in good shape, and it was a pleasure to have such a gorgeous guy in her bed.

He pushed himself up to take off his tie and jacket, but she pulled him down before he could rid himself off the shirt. "Keep it on," she whispered, and kissed him, and he laughed and shifted on top of her, pressing her into the mattress.

"Hard and fast?" he said.

"Mmm…" She couldn't think of anything better.

Withdrawing his wallet from his back pocket, he took out a condom, thank God, sat back, and undid his belt and zipper. Roberta watched him release the erection that had obviously been begging to set free, and holy moly, it was as long and hard as she'd hoped, making her clench deep inside.

She closed a hand around him and gave him a few strokes, enjoying the way the breath hissed between his teeth. It wasn't long before he moved her away, rolled the condom on, then positioned himself back between her legs. Pushing up her skirt, he gently pulled her panties to one side.

"Fuck," he said, inhaling at his first sight of her. She watched, face warming, as he slid his thumb down into her folds, gathered some moisture, and spread it up to her clit. He tipped his head to the side as he circled his thumb over the swollen button, and she moaned and tilted her hips up to help him, loving the way his eyelids had slipped to half-mast, his eyes taking on a sultry, sexy look.

Maneuvering the tip of his erection to her entrance, he then lowered himself on top of her. Keeping his gaze on hers, he pushed his hips forward.

Roberta groaned as he moved inside her, conscious of him pulling back, then easing forward until he was fully sheathed.

"All right?" he said, kissing her lips, her cheek, her closed eyelids.

"Mmm. You feel… amazing."

"You too." He started to move, slow, regular thrusts until he was coated with her moisture, and then faster, harder. Pushing up her top, he lowered his mouth to her breast again, and she spiraled into dreamy blissfulness as her body began its inexorable journey to a climax.

Outside, the wind howled and the rain beat on the glass, but it only seemed to add to their passion. Jasmine the cat had long since jumped down from the bed, and Roberta was aware of the lamp flickering on the bedside table as, in the distance, lightning flashed and thunder rolled around the hills.

Despite it being the middle of winter, the room had grown warm, and beneath his shirt, Angus's skin was hot and slick. *Aaahhh*, God, this was amazing. But more, she wanted more. She stroked down his back, then tucked her hands beneath his trousers and the elastic of his boxers, squeezing the tight muscles of his butt before giving one a sound smack with the palm of her hand.

He slowed and gave her a wry look.

"Harder," she said.

"I don't want to hurt you."

"I won't break. Come on, Angus. You want to fuck me properly, don't you?"

Thunder rolled again, making her jump, and Angus laughed. "You're not afraid of taking what you want, are you?"

"No. *Aaahhh*, I ache. Come on, please."

He lifted up onto his hands so he was plunging down into her, and gave several long, slow thrusts, maybe making sure she could take all of him and that he wasn't going to hurt her. When she moaned and wrapped her legs around his waist, he muttered something under his breath, then started to thrust properly, deep and hard, making the headboard bang against the wall.

"Yes," she cried out, "oh fuck, yes. Harder."

So he did, riding her hard, and she hung onto the headboard with both hands, letting her knees fall wide and giving herself over to him. Her climax crashed over her along with the thunder, everything inside clenching and pulsing multiple times, exquisite sensations rippling through her. She was conscious of saying his name, of yelling yes over and over again, and then he was coming too, his body stiffening, muscles hardening, as his hips jerked and he spilled inside her.

At that moment, lightning flashed, thunder crashed immediately, and the lamp on the table went out.

"Jesus." He collapsed on top of her, breathing heavily. "Did we do that?"

Roberta started laughing, and he joined in. She couldn't stop the giggles rising inside her, and he winced and withdrew, then fell onto his back, his deep laughter shaking his whole body.

She curled up beside him, still laughing, and he gathered her in his arms and pressed a kiss on her hair.

They lay like that for a long while, as their breathing slowed and their bodies cooled. Roberta didn't ever want to move. She wanted to stay there for the rest of her life, in that warm room, with his hand tracing patterns on her back, and her body still humming with the echoes of her pleasure.

"Thank you," she told him eventually, more grateful than he'd ever know that he hadn't just walked away from her. "I needed that."

"Glad to be of service." His voice sounded a tad wry.

She lifted up a little and rested her chin on his chest. "I didn't mean you were literally the first port in a storm."

"I know."

"You weren't just convenient, Angus."

"It's okay." He pulled her up so he could kiss her. "It's been a tough week, and a hell of a day. We both needed to let some tension go."

"Anyway," she said playfully, "it is legal. We are married."

He didn't say anything to that, and she cursed herself silently. Why had she mentioned it?

"I should go," he said, lifting onto an elbow.

They studied each other for a moment. She'd told him that she didn't expect anything more than this, and she'd meant it. What had she thought would happen? That he'd declare his love for her, announce that he thought they should stay married, and move in tomorrow?

Grow up, she told herself. She'd had some great sex with a guy she liked a lot. Not everyone was as lucky as that. She had to count her blessings and move on.

"Thank you," she said genuinely.

His lips curved up, and he raised a hand to trace a finger down her nose. "You're welcome."

"Angus..." She hesitated.

"What?" His blue eyes were clear, warm with affection.

"We can still be friends, can't we? It won't make things weird."

He frowned. "Of course we can. You're one of my best friends."

"Please don't regret what we've done. I'd hate it if that happened."

"I don't," he said. He rolled over, stood, and started to button up his shirt.

Roberta pushed herself up and tried to tidy her appearance, doing up her bra behind her back on one hook, and straightening her skirt. When she stood and turned, he was slipping on his jacket.

She wanted to ask him to stay for a drink, but she was convinced he'd turn her down, and she didn't want to have to face the rejection. Instead, she led the way out of her bedroom and down to the living room, bumping into the sofa in the dark because all the lamps had gone out in the power outage. Cursing, she grabbed her iPad and switched it on, giving them both some light.

The thunder had abated, although it was still raining hard. Normally, she would have suggested he stay until the storm had passed, but again she didn't want him to turn her down. So she walked with him to the door, and stopped and smiled.

"Thank you," she said again. "I appreciate you bringing me home, and for… keeping me entertained."

He gave a soft laugh and stepped closer to her. "I have a feeling it was always going to happen. There's been tension between us for a long time."

"I thought I was the only one feeling it," she said honestly.

He tucked a strand of her hair behind her ear. "No. I've wanted you since day one. But as I said, my life is complicated at the moment, and there's no room in it for love."

She wanted to ask him what he meant, to beg him to tell her, but she didn't want to make a fool of herself. "All right."

"I'd better go."

"We need to talk about the certificate at some point," she said as he opened the door. "We might have lost it in the crash, but we're still married. We ought to do something about that."

He looked out at the rain, then gave her a quick smile. "Yeah. We will."

Leaning forward, he gave her a quick, hard kiss. Then, turning up his collar, he jogged off into the darkness toward his car. The headlights came on, the car pulled away, and she watched the rear lights disappearing into the distance.

She went inside, shut the door, and walked into the living room. It was cool there, and dark. Her spirits sank slowly, like ash from a bonfire caught in the wind.

She'd asked him not to regret it tonight, but she was certain he would. And now that the storm had passed, she regretted it too. At the time, she'd wanted him more than anything in the world, but now all she could think was that she'd have to face him tomorrow, and they needed to sort out the Vegas wedding, and it was all such a fucking mess.

There were no tears left inside her, though, so she just sank onto the sofa, welcoming Jasmine onto her lap as she jumped up. And she stayed there for a long time, looking out into the darkness as the rain lashed at the windows.

Chapter Eleven

Angus had a lot on his plate. He had an extremely hectic day job that was very rarely nine-to-five, and a busy social life. The pressure of looking after Katrina and little Katie was always at the back of his mind, too. This was why, he told himself, he hadn't yet confronted the issue of his marriage to Roberta.

There were far more important things to think about. Having sex with her had been amazing, but it had been a one-off, and it was time to put her out of his mind.

His body took a bit longer to get the memo, and when he got into bed and turned out the lights it was impossible not to replay images of her in his mind, with her bright green eyes, her smooth tanned skin, and her soft lips that had parted as she'd come, crying out his name. He couldn't deny the feelings of wistfulness and longing that rose within him, with regret topping them both. He wished they could take the relationship further.

But he turned over and forced himself to recite the two-hundred-and-six bones in the human body until his erection went away, and eventually he fell asleep.

The following day, he awoke clear-headed, refreshed, and determined. A few years ago, he'd made his choice knowing full well what the outcome would be, and he couldn't start crying about it now. Okay, so maybe he hadn't planned on meeting Roberta, but he wasn't sixteen anymore, running on raw emotions all the time. He was adult enough to know that life wasn't all about love and sex. It was also about loyalty and commitment and doing what was right, and not sleeping with Roberta again was definitely the right thing to do.

So he rose and went to his Saturday morning surgery until lunchtime, made a few home visits to patients who couldn't make it into the surgery, then went to the gym and did a full workout, pushing his body hard. After that, he went home, showered and changed, and made himself a sandwich as he checked his phone. There was a text from his mother asking if he'd remembered to send his father a sixtieth birthday card. One from Katrina asking him if she should worry about a rash on Katie's chest. And one was from Elliot.

I've left you a few PlayStation games at the Brides shop, Elliot said.

Angus texted his mother and said yes, he had bought a card, then texted Katrina and told her not to worry, that kids have rashes all the time, but to keep an eye on her temperature and to let him know if her condition changed in any way.

Then he sat back and pursed his lips. PlayStation games were his one little weakness, mainly because they allowed him to escape. While he was playing, he couldn't think of anything else—and he could really do with them right now, bearing in mind that it was taking every ounce of his concentration not to think about Roberta.

Of course, calling in at the Brides shop would probably mean seeing her in the café. But maybe she'd have gone home early or be serving customers, and she might not even see him.

He'd risk it. Elliot had recently bought and finished the latest Assassin's Creed, and he was desperate to escape to Ancient Egypt and fight some bad guys.

He wasn't going because he wanted to see Roberta. Not at all.

He drove the short distance from his house in Waipapa to town, parked behind the Post Office, and walked along to the high street.

It was late afternoon, and the small town was growing quieter, most people having finished their shopping, while it was too early for the restaurants to serve dinner. He passed the chemist, the clothing boutiques, and the little shops selling gifts like jade necklaces in the shapes of koru spirals and fish hooks, and crossed over the road to Bay of Islands Brides.

The Goldsmith girls had done an amazing job with the place, he thought as he approached. The only bridal shop in Kerikeri, it was frequently filled not only by those planning their upcoming weddings, but also by women who came into the café ostensibly for coffee but secretly wanting to admire the gowns that glittered in the light from the chandelier.

He supposed he could see why women loved weddings. Every little girl wants to be a princess, he thought, sure that little Katie would be no different. It was the one day in a woman's lifetime when she got to wear a ballgown and be center stage for the day. No wonder they liked to make such a fuss about it. As a guy, he didn't find the pomp and ceremony appealing at all.

And yet... he paused by the front window and looked up at the sleek gown behind the glass. He could imagine Roberta in something like this, her hair pinned up with curls falling around her face, a sparkling tiara holding a lacy veil in place. How would it feel to have her standing beside him, to place his ring on her finger to tell other men she was his? To have her pledge in front of their friends, family, and maybe even God to love him until 'death parts us'?

Of course, they'd already done that in Vegas, even though he couldn't remember it. He pursed his lips. There'd been no ring, and there was no certificate. Even so, a sliver of ice ran down his back.

He glared at the gown and pushed the shop door open.

"Angus!" Noelle stood by one of the mannequins, holding a dress that had practically engulfed her with its layers and layers of petticoats.

"Hey." He smiled and walked in. "Do you need a hand?"

"Oh, please. This one kind of got away from me a bit."

Checking that his hands were clean—he'd hate to get dirt on the pristine-white gown—he picked up the hanger and raised the dress so she could lift the petticoats over the mannequin's head. Then they lowered the dress together until it sat comfortably on the mannequin's body.

"Phew!" Noelle stood back and admired their handiwork. "That's better. Thank you."

"Mighty Angus to the rescue!"

"Your superhero is named after a McDonald's burger?" He gave her a wry look, and she grinned. "What can I do for you today, Dr. McGregor?"

"Elliot said he'd left some games here for me."

"Ah, yes. Boys and their toys." She smiled. "They're in my office. Come with me."

He followed her through the shop, past the rows of sparkling white and cream shoes, the tiaras, everything studded with gemstones and sequins. What was it with girls and sparkly stuff?

Stopping at the door to Noelle's office, he waited as she retrieved the bag. He liked Roberta's mother. As her doctor, he had an insight into the life behind the bubbly persona she projected. He knew she'd struggled since losing her husband to a heart attack, although she'd gone to a grief counsellor, which seemed to have helped her a bit. He wondered if she would ever meet another man. How old was she? Fifty-one? Fifty-two? It was a difficult age to start dating again, not that any age was easy. But she was slap bang in the middle of the menopause and struggling with all the usual effects of mid-life, both mental and physical. Still, she was slender and quite beautiful with her stunning silver hair. She'd aged well. Surely there was an unattached man out there who could provide companionship and love?

"Here you go." She retrieved the bag from behind her desk and brought it over to him.

"Thanks."

"I can see what you'll be doing tonight."

"Running through Cairo, hopefully," he said, extracting the Assassin's Creed game and grinning.

"Well say hello to Tutankhamun from me."

He laughed. "Will do. Thanks." He turned to go.

"Angus?"

He stopped and glanced back. "Yeah?"

"I haven't had a chance to get you alone yet, but I just wanted to say… I'm glad you're okay. That you made it back." Her eyes glistened, and he knew she was thinking about Mike. "Roberta told me about what you did on the plane, how you helped all those injured passengers, and what you did for Libby. She thought you were amazing, and said it would have been a thousand times worse without you there. We're very lucky to have you, Angus."

Taken aback, he blinked and smiled. "That's a lovely thing to say. Thank you."

"My girls have been very lucky with their friends. If you were ever to become… more than that, I wouldn't be disappointed."

He stared at her. She raised her eyebrows.

His lips twitched. "Noelle Goldsmith, are you playing Cupid?"

"Wouldn't dream of it."

"I feel as if I've stepped out of *Pride and Prejudice*. Which of your lovely daughters are you thinking of matching me with?"

She smiled. "You really have to ask me that?"

Had Roberta told her mother about the fake marriage? He hoped not, because that would make things even more complicated.

Noelle's smile faded. "I'm teasing you," she said softly, placing her hand on his arm. "I didn't mean to interfere."

"It's just… complicated for me." He teetered on the verge of telling her more; there was something about her gentle smile and friendly manner that made him want to confide in her. But in the end, he just sighed. "I'm not in the dating arena at the moment. If I were, I assure you, Roberta would be at the top of my list."

Her curious gaze surveyed him, but all she said was, "Okay. You're such a serious boy. All work and no play, remember?"

"Well, I haven't been called a boy for about fifteen years, so thank you for that."

"Men are just boys with bigger toys," she scoffed, pointing at the bag of PlayStation games in his hand.

"Fair enough." He winked at her. "I'll see you later."

"Are you going to the party tomorrow?"

He nodded. It was Rafe's thirtieth birthday, and he and Phoebe were throwing a party at their house for their friends and family. "I'm guessing Libby's not going."

"I doubt it. Roberta will know. She told Libby to take as much time off work at the café as she wanted, but Libby said she wants to keep busy, so she'll be back in on Monday." She held his gaze. "Life's short, Angus. *Carpe diem.*"

He gave a short laugh and walked away.

When he passed the archway leading to the café, he had no intention of stopping. The Assassin's Creed game was burning a hole in the bag and he'd already decided he was going to pick up a pizza and game the night away.

But he couldn't stop himself glancing into the café, and his feet slowed automatically to a halt.

Roberta stood in the middle of the room, leaning over a table as she cleaned it. She wore black leggings that made her legs look as if they went all the way to her armpits, and a flesh-colored tee that, for a moment, made him think she was topless.

Man, she had a great bottom. Perfectly shaped, *tight as*, with just enough muscle for a guy to hold onto.

It was a short step to imagining her without the leggings, her thighs and bottom bare as they had been in the hotel room in Vegas, and him sliding inside her from behind.

Wow. In approximately two seconds he had a hard-on the size of the Eiffel Tower. All the blood in his body had rushed to his groin so fast that he felt dizzy.

She happened to turn at that moment and caught sight of him in the doorway. Her eyes widened, she inhaled sharply, and he swore he saw her nipples tighten through the cotton tee.

Carpe the crap out of every diem, McGregor.

Chapter Twelve

"Hey." Roberta adopted a nonchalant pose, dropping a hip, resting one hand on it. Had her shock been obvious? Hopefully he hadn't realized what an effect he had on her.

"Busy day?" He stepped down into the café and walked slowly up to her. He wore black jeans and a gray T-shirt that bore the slogan 'Doctor—because superhero isn't an official job title.'

"Please tell me you didn't buy the T-shirt for yourself," she said.

He looked down at it and laughed. "I didn't even read it when I took it out of the drawer. Nah, a friend bought it for me."

"A girl friend?"

He just smiled.

She wished she hadn't asked. It was none of her business.

But he looked so gorgeous today. She'd spent all night dreaming about him, as if her very cells retained the memory of his touch, his presence lingering in her room like aftershave. She'd just managed to convince herself it had all meant nothing and was purely physical, and now here he was, his eyes filled with enough warmth to turn her to caramel inside.

"Just passing?" she asked.

He indicated the bag under his arm. "Picking up something Elliot left for me."

So he hadn't come here to see her. But he was a well-mannered guy and thought it would be polite to say hi to the girl he'd shagged the night before.

That stung. "Don't let me keep you," she said, a little crossly.

Angus's gaze slid down her. "That top makes you look semi-naked."

Her eyebrows rose. "What?"

Cathy, one of Noelle's friends who helped out behind the counter from time to time, stared at him, and he pursed his lips. "Sorry, did I say that out loud?"

Cathy laughed. Roberta snorted. "Come here," she told him, tugging his arm and leading him out of the shop.

She let the door close behind them. The sunshine turned the ends of his short brown hair to gold, making it look as if he had a halo. Yeah right. He was a long way from being angelic.

"You are trouble," she told him.

"Yeah, I know." He smiled. "I wasn't going to bother you, but you were leaning over the table, and you're wearing leggings, and I kind of lost the plot."

Her lips curved up. "I think there's a compliment in there somewhere."

"There most definitely is."

For a long moment, they just studied each other.

It was the middle of winter now, but the sub-tropical Northland sun was still warm on her skin. The cool breeze sent the last few leaves fluttering from the skeletal tree on the corner, while the smell of incense blew from the hippie shop a few doors down. A car drove past them, music drifting through its open window, a very old song; Dinah Washington, if she was correct, explaining that she was *Mad About the Boy*.

They'd been standing there too long, saying nothing, but her mind had gone blank at his compliment, and his eyes were the same color as the autumn sky behind him.

"Are you going to the party tomorrow?" he asked.

Of course, it was Rafe's thirtieth birthday. He and Phoebe had planned a party weeks ago. They'd come close to cancelling it, feeling it was inappropriate to celebrate after the horrific week they'd just had, but Libby had told them they absolutely had to go ahead. She'd explained that even though she wouldn't be going this time, she wanted everyone to enjoy themselves.

"Yes," Roberta said. "I'll be there."

"Maybe we should have a dance or something. For old time's sake."

"Maybe." She couldn't tear her eyes away from his. If he'd only been interested in a one-night stand, why was he looking at her like that? Why hadn't he walked out of the shop with barely a glance?

"I dreamt about you last night," he murmured. "All night, I think. I'm knackered."

She bit her lip. "Me too."

"It was pretty special, wasn't it?" His gaze slid to her lips, which parted involuntarily.

"Um… yes. It was." Her heart was racing. She should say it was a great evening but it was over now, and they shouldn't mention it again. They needed to draw a line underneath what happened in Vegas and both get on with their lives.

His eyes came back to hers, and she could tell by the look in them that he was thinking about what she looked like naked.

"I'll see you tomorrow," he said, softly, lazily, a hint of a smile on his lips.

"Okay." Her voice was little more than a squeak.

Angus slid his hands into his pockets and walked away, casting her a final glance over his shoulder before he disappeared around the corner.

Roberta inhaled a deep, shaky breath, then blew it out as she went back into the café, where she discovered her mother and Cathy standing by the counter, watching her.

"Wow, that was intense," Cathy said. "That look the two of you were sharing could have turned sand to glass."

Noelle raised her eyebrows. "I have to admit, she's right."

Roberta scowled. "Give it a rest."

"He's a doctor, he's gorgeous, and he's single," Noelle said. "I think you might be setting your sights a bit too high."

"It's not me. He's not interested, Mum. He told me as much."

"Men don't know what they want until they have it," Noelle advised her. "He's got the hots for you."

"Mum!"

"He has. It's obvious." She glanced at Cathy, who nodded vehemently. "And you shouldn't take no for an answer. He'll come around."

"I don't want to stalk a guy until he's ready to 'come around'," Roberta snapped, putting air quotes around the words. "For once, I'd like it if a man was into me." She stopped, her throat tightening. Her mother knew what she'd been through with Ian. Couldn't she understand that it didn't matter how much she and Angus were attracted to one another; if he wasn't prepared to make an effort for her, she didn't want to get involved?

Cathy turned away to take some plates out to the kitchen.

"All right," Noelle said, rubbing her daughter's arm. "I'm sorry. That was unfair."

"I can't do it again, Mum," Roberta whispered, looking out at the leaves dancing along the pavement. "I can't get involved with someone who won't give me one-hundred percent."

"I do understand, sweetheart, but you can't tar everyone with the same brush. You have to take a chance on love sometimes."

Love? That didn't fit into this at all. The various emotions she'd felt so far in their relationship, such as it was, were like the ingredients needed to make Tiramisu, and love was like a tiny red-hot chili—it didn't fit in the recipe at all. Maybe, if he'd been interested, their physical attraction could have developed into something else, but he'd told her directly there was no room in his life for love.

"I've got things to do," she said, fed up with thinking about it.

"All right." Noelle knew when to back off, and she returned to the bridal shop to start packing up for the end of the day.

Roberta returned to cleaning the tables, determined to put Angus McGregor out of her mind. If he came to the party, maybe they could have a dance, but then she'd turn her back on him politely and spend the rest of her time talking with her friends and family. She refused to waste her time betting on another horse that wasn't even going to make it out of the gate.

*

Just after four p.m. the next day, she turned the car onto Rafe and Phoebe's road and parked behind Bianca's car. It was another beautiful winter's afternoon, the sky clear of clouds, the sun warm, but with a bite to the wind when it blew across the inlet.

Roberta walked up the drive, glancing around for Angus's car and not finding it. She wasn't sure whether to feel upset or relieved. Deciding to make it the latter, she walked around the side of the house and discovered everyone seated on the deck, with music playing from the speakers and drinks being poured and passed around. As well as her friends and family, there were firefighters and their families from the station where Rafe worked, and various other faces she'd seen around town.

A cheer went up as her family saw her. She waved hello, hugged Phoebe, and passed her the bottle of wine she'd brought.

"Ooh, Blue Penguin Bay," Phoebe said, reading the label. "They do a lovely Chardonnay. Do you want a glass?"

"Maybe later." Roberta smiled as Rafe came up. "Hello, birthday boy."

"Hey." He kissed her on the cheek. "Thanks for coming."

"Aw, wouldn't have missed it for the world." She took a seat by Elliot and Karen, and gave Rafe a grin. "So what's it like, turning the big three-oh?"

"Similar to being twenty-nine, funnily enough." He cracked open a beer and took a swig.

"I can't believe I'm married to an old man," Phoebe said.

"Steady on," Dominic said. "If he's old, that makes me ancient."

"If the cap fits."

Elliot laughed. "I'm not saying anything. We're all heading that way."

"Over a year for me yet," Roberta said.

"Ages for me and Bianca," Phoebe pointed out.

"Well I'm thirty in November," Elliot said.

"That means Libby must be thirty in December," Roberta said.

"Yeah." Elliot's smile faded.

"How is she doing?" Fliss asked. "I'm guessing she's not coming tonight."

"No," Roberta said. "I don't think she's quite ready for a big party. But I was thinking about having the girls over next weekend. We could have a slumber party and paint each other's toenails."

"I'd rather go to that party," Rafe said.

Everyone laughed, except Elliot. As the conversation moved on, Roberta studied her brother, who was looking out at the river, unusually quiet. Next to him, Karen glanced at him, then rolled her eyes and turned away to talk to someone on her left. Roberta frowned. What was going on there?

She had no time to think about it further, because Rafe cheered and several others joined in, and she turned in her chair to see that Angus had arrived.

Heat rushed up through her, warming her face, and she looked away hastily. Her eyes met Dominic's, and his eyebrows rose with amusement, so she knew she must have turned scarlet.

"Excuse me," she mumbled, and rose to go over to the drinks table. What was wrong with her? The slumber party had been a joke, she scolded herself. It didn't mean she had to act like a teenager.

After pouring herself a soda, she mingled for a while, saying hello to the other guests, many of whom frequented her café. The party was warming up; people were dancing to the music, and Phoebe and Bianca served up a huge pot of chili and rice and left everyone to help themselves. Drink flowed along with the food, which naturally aided the atmosphere.

Not sure if she was in the mood for the spicy food, Roberta finished her conversation with one of the female firefighters and then got herself another drink. Leaning on the balustrade that ran around the deck, she shivered a little in the cool early evening breeze and sipped her soda.

She felt an odd sense of dislocation; a heightened awareness of little details, as if she was observing herself from the outside. Most people present had been to Mike's funeral, and to her ears their laughter seemed forced, as if they were all trying to pretend they were unaffected by his absence. It felt wrong, Libby not being there, and even though she'd insisted Rafe should go ahead with the party, Roberta felt uncomfortable, as if she was betraying her friend. In the old days, everyone would have been in mourning and dressed in black for months, and at that moment she could understand why. Death was swept under the carpet nowadays—it was an inconvenience that nobody wanted to think about. Out of sight, out of mind.

"Are you okay?"

Startled out of her reverie, she looked up at the gorgeous doctor who'd snuck up on her and who was now watching her with concern.

"A tad melancholy," she said, forcing a smile on her face. "Nothing to worry about."

"You thinking about Mike?"

"Yeah. And Libby. It seems wrong somehow to be enjoying yourself, you know? When she's so sad."

"Life goes on," he said. "Worst cliché ever."

"Yeah."

Phoebe had placed citronella candles around the deck to ward off any insects. The flames danced in Angus's eyes, entrancing her. How she wished she could just take his hand and say, "Let's go home." Return with him to her house, pour themselves a drink, and curl up in bed together. She tore her gaze away and looked out at the darkening river. Not all fairy tales had happy endings.

Chapter Thirteen

Angus studied the pale face of the girl who'd been in his thoughts almost twenty-four-seven for days.

He'd always thought of her as spirited and carefree, but it was becoming obvious to him that her nonchalant attitude hid a sensitive soul that, for whatever reason, was struggling with the recent death of one of their friends. That, in itself, wasn't necessarily something to worry about; as a doctor, he would rarely put a patient on antidepressants when someone close to them had died, believing that grief was a natural process that couldn't be cured by medication. But sometimes a shock like the one they'd had could be the catalyst in something more serious. He would've been surprised if everyone in the crash *hadn't* suffered from PTSD to some extent. But it was how each person dealt with it that would be the most important thing.

"Want some food?" he suggested. "It might make you feel better."

"No thanks." She sipped her soda and flicked him a smile. "I'm okay; I don't need supervision."

"Who said anything about supervision? I was hoping for a dance." He'd waited for something slow and sensual to come on, and now Beyoncé was singing *Crazy in Love* in the sexy way she had for the Fifty Shades movie, and Angus wanted to take away Roberta's unhappiness and make her smile again.

He took her drink from her hand and placed it on the table. She gave a troubled sigh. "Angus…"

"Dance with me." He pulled her gently toward him, cupped her hand in his, slid his right hand onto her waist, and began moving to the music.

Her fingers curled around his, and her body swayed automatically, even though she protested, "I'm tired."

"Just one song," he said.

She sighed again, and then, unbidden, she moved closer to him and rested her cheek on his shoulder. Surprised, he curled their hands in close to his chest, his other hand keeping her tight against him.

He hadn't expected this. She was warm in his arms, and her hair smelled of strawberries, making him think of long summer nights, and how wonderful it would be to slide with her beneath cotton sheets.

Why did he feel so protective toward her? She was in her late twenties, she lived alone, she ran her own business, and she hardly needed looking after. But there was something vulnerable about her—was he the only one who saw it?

He glanced over at where her family and their friends sat eating, wondering if they'd noticed the two of them dancing. But they were all engrossed in their food and conversation, and besides, he and Roberta were just good friends. Nobody would think there was anything more to this than a few minutes of companionship. Nobody would guess the feelings stirring in his belly at that moment.

His fingers splaying at the base of her spine, he brushed her back with his thumb, remembering how it had felt to slide his hand beneath her top to cup her breasts. He wished he'd spent more time when they'd had sex arousing her, playing with her, but need had taken over for both of them, a hunger that could only be assuaged one way.

She stirred in his arms, sighing. Her lips were at the base of his throat, and he felt her breath whisper across there, making him shiver.

Moving back a little, she looked up into his eyes. "I know you have no time for love," she whispered. "But what about sex?"

His eyes widened. "What do you mean?"

"Do you want me, Angus?"

His brow furrowed. "You know I do."

"I'm going to the bathroom. Not the main one—the *en suite* off the master bedroom. Wait a minute, then follow me there."

Dropping his hand, she turned and walked away, disappearing into the house.

Angus stood there, dumbfounded, his heart racing. Was she suggesting what he thought she was suggesting? Surely not… here? In Rafe and Phoebe's home?

He couldn't. It was a daft idea; someone would walk in on them, and it would be embarrassing, mortifying even. He couldn't afford for this—what was it? affair? fling?—to become common knowledge, not right now.

But his heart was banging its fists on his ribs, and the thought of having her in his arms again was overriding all his safety precautions, bypassing his firewalls. Of their own accord, his feet began moving toward the house, but he made himself take time, circling behind those standing chatting by the food, trying not to draw attention to himself. But nobody noticed or even glanced his way, and he went into the living room, then down the darkened corridor that he knew led toward the master bedroom.

He couldn't do this… it was crazy. He felt feverish, despite the cool temperature. Perhaps he was coming down with something. Or perhaps it was just desire coursing through his veins; he felt dizzy with it, all the blood in his body rushing to his groin.

He slipped into Rafe and Phoebe's bedroom, then across to the *en suite* bathroom. He ran both hands through his hair, bit his lip, then knocked lightly on the door.

It opened, and Roberta reached out, grabbed his shirt, and pulled him inside.

She'd left the light off, and the room was in semi-darkness, her face in shadow. She didn't say anything, so Angus locked the door behind him, then turned to face her.

"I wasn't sure if you'd come," she whispered.

"I can't say no to you."

She moved closer to him and rested her hands on his chest. "I know this is wrong, but I can't stop thinking about you."

"It's not wrong, it's just… unwise, probably. But right now, I don't care." He held her face in his hands and touched his lips to hers.

Roberta gave a half laugh, half sob, and then lifted her arms around his neck, leaning into the kiss. Angus lowered his arms around her, feeling her soft breasts pressing against his chest. He slid his hands down onto her bottom, pulling her toward him so she could be in no doubt as to how much he wanted her.

A moan sounded low in her throat, and she plunged her tongue into his mouth, clenching her fingers in his hair. "I want you," she whispered against his lips.

"I want you too."

"Right now."

He lifted his head to look at her briefly. "You're sure?"

She nodded, and he felt a rush of pleasure that she desired him so much she couldn't wait.

Turning her so her back was to the wall, he kissed her while he gathered up her long black skirt in the fingers of his right hand. His heart increased its pace as he revealed the knee-length black boots clinging to her shapely calves. "Yowza."

She gave a soft laugh, which turned into a gasp as he stroked a hand up her bare thigh. Sliding it beneath the elastic of her panties, he moved his fingers down, into the heart of her.

"Mmm." She tipped her head back on the door and closed her eyes as she lifted her leg around his hips to give him better access.

Angus rested his forearm on the door above her head and touched his lips to hers while he stroked her. Man, she was already swollen and slippery, and the hot breath of her sighs whispered across his lips as he swirled his finger over her clit.

"One of these days," he told her, his voice husky with desire, "I'm going to get you into a bed and make love to you properly, without rushing."

"Oh, I don't mind hard and fast," she whispered back. "In fact… mmm… it might be my… favorite… *aaahhh…*"

He'd moved his fingers beneath and slid them inside her, and she arched against him as he curled them and stroked firmly. "You're so fucking hot," he said, conscious of her bare thigh and her black boot locked around his waist.

"Mmm… Angus…" Her eyelids fluttered.

As quickly as he could, he retrieved a condom from his wallet. Then he undid his jeans, pulled down his boxers, and rolled the condom on. In those few seconds, she divested herself of her panties.

"Where do you want me?" she said, tossing them aside.

He turned her around so she was holding onto the basin, and moved her legs backward so she was bent at the waist. Then he lifted up her skirt, revealing her bare legs and black boots. "Oh yeah." This was just how he'd pictured her when he'd seen her in the café, bending over the table. The boots were an added bonus.

She widened her stance and glanced over her shoulder at him. Her eyes glittered in the moonlight coming through the window, and her lips parted. He guided his erection beneath her, sliding it through her folds to gather some of her moisture, then pressed the tip against her entrance. She tilted her hips, and he pushed forward and sheathed himself inside her wet warmth.

"Fuck." She dropped her head. "Oh Jesus."

He slid a hand up her sweater and flicked open the catch on her bra. The elastic gave, and he moved both hands around her ribs to cup her breasts. They filled his palms like soft fruit, the nipples hard in his fingers, and when he tugged on them, she moaned and pushed back against him.

Slowly, he began to thrust, the sensation of plunging into her flesh almost too much to bear. "You feel fucking amazing," he murmured, one hand continuing to tease her nipples, while he slid the other hand down so he could continue to arouse her clit.

"Ohhh…" She let out a long moan, pushing back when he thrust so their flesh met with a sharp slap.

"Ah, Roberta…" This was so fucking decadent, snatching time together as if they were teenagers, driven purely by their physical desires.

Yeah, Angus, there's no emotion behind this at all. You keep telling yourself that and you might begin to believe it.

He thrust hard, closing his eyes, and concentrated on the sensation of being inside her, of her clamping around him when he tried to slide back, and sucking him in when he moved forward. It felt amazing. Her breasts swung beneath the sweater, and her hands tightened on the basin, her breaths turning ragged.

"Oh jeez," she said.

Holding her hips, he pounded into her until they were both coming, clenching hard, bodies locked in a blissful paroxysm. He gritted his teeth so he didn't cry out, and Roberta covered her mouth with a hand, but it was impossible to stop every grunt, every cry, and by the time they'd finished, they were both trying not to laugh.

"Shit." He leaned on the basin, his hands either side of hers, and lowered his lips to her shoulder. "That was intense."

She turned her head, her green eyes finding his, and he kissed her, long and slow.

Eventually, he withdrew, flushed the condom, and zipped himself up. Roberta found her underwear and pulled it on, then straightened her clothing.

Finally, he pulled her into his arms, and they stood there for a while, with the moonlight streaming over them, while their hearts slowed down.

Already, Angus began to feel some regret. Not at having sex with her, because he could never regret that, but at the manner in which they'd done it. She deserved so much more than this. She was grieving and looking for comfort; he should have been the bigger man and bought her a tub of ice cream or something.

But then maybe, he thought, he was grieving and looking for comfort too. It was the first time he considered that, actually, he might be suffering from a little PTSD as well. And what was more natural when you've looked death in the face than to prove to yourself that you're alive and stimulate all your senses with some really good sex?

"Don't regret it," Roberta whispered as if reading his thoughts.

"I don't. I won't, I swear." He kissed the top of her head. "I just feel that I've made a mess of everything. But I will sort it. I promise."

She nodded and moved back. "I suppose we'd better go."

"I'll go first if you like. I'll go out the front and pretend I was getting something from my car."

"All right."

He slid a knuckle beneath her chin, lifted her face, and kissed her. Then he unlocked the bathroom door, peeked out, and slipped into the night.

Chapter Fourteen

Three days later

Roberta sat in the waiting room and flicked through a magazine.

She had no idea what she was looking at; the photos of celebrities caught on holiday in their bikinis or showing off their multi-million-dollar houses held no interest for her. But hopefully it made her look as if she wasn't nervous.

It didn't stop her emotions jangling around inside her like charms on a bracelet, though. Maybe this was a mistake. When she'd had sex with Angus at the birthday party on Sunday, she'd propositioned him, so of course he wasn't going to say no. Free sex! What guy would refuse that? But even though he'd asked her to dance first, it hadn't meant anything. He hadn't said he wanted to see her again.

She was reading between the lines, but what if the words she assumed were there in invisible ink turned out to be all in her head? She didn't think Angus was the sort of guy who'd use women, but equally he was a man, and no doubt thought with his dick first and his brain second. He'd probably regretted the sex as soon as he'd walked away. He—

"Ms. Goldsmith?"

Her head jerked up at his soft voice. He stood at the edge of the waiting room, watching her, a soft smile on his lips.

Swallowing hard, she put down the magazine, shouldered her bag, and followed him along the corridor.

As they approached his room, he opened the door and stood to one side to let her enter first. She brushed past him, the smell of his aftershave filling her nostrils as she did so, something subtle but seductive that stirred her up and sent her emotions jangling again.

Control yourself, girl!

"Hello," he said, closing the door behind them. "Didn't expect to see your name on the appointment list for this afternoon. If you'd wanted to see me, you could have just rung me." He walked toward her, a wry smile on his lips.

She cleared her throat. "Actually, I'm here to see you as my doctor."

His eyebrows rose. "Oh." Clearly, he hadn't expected that. "Am I your doctor?"

"You're the doctor for all our family."

"I don't think I've ever seen you in an official capacity before though, have I?" He gestured to the chair by his desk and sat in his seat.

"I'm never sick," she said, taking the patient chair.

He studied her for a moment. "You don't have to see me, Roberta. I can find out if one of the other doctors is available for you."

"No, it's okay," she said. "We're still friends, aren't we?"

His brow furrowed. "Of course."

"I don't want to talk to anyone else," she said. How could she explain that despite everything that was going on between them, she still trusted him more than anyone? "It's not… intimate or anything," she added.

"Might be worth me giving you a once-over anyway," he said with a grin. Then he looked slightly shocked. "Sorry, my mouth keeps saying things before I've had a chance to think them through."

She chuckled. "Are you like this with all your patients?"

"No, of course not. There's something about you that loosens my tongue."

The thought of his loose tongue sliding down her body gave her goosebumps.

He gave her a wry look and leaned back in his chair. "You've glazed over."

"Of course I have," she said with exasperation. "You can't drag a girl off to have raunchy sex in the bathroom and then expect her to act all normal next time you meet."

"You dragged me," he pointed out, smiling.

"Yeah, well, you didn't need a lot of persuading."

"No, I didn't." His eyes were warm. "What can I do for you today, Roberta?"

Her humor faded away, and she looked down at her hands. "I just want some advice. You mentioned PTSD, and I wondered whether that's what I'm suffering from, and whether I should do anything about it."

"Okay." He leaned forward and clasped his hands together. "What symptoms do you have?"

Now she was here, she wasn't sure how to describe it. "I don't feel like… myself."

"In what way?"

"The crash, and what happened to Mike… it changed me, Angus, and not in a good way. I've always been fearless and bold, like the knight in that poem, what was it called?"

"I've no idea."

"When a knight won his spurs, although it was gallant and bold, not fearless."

"Right. Are you nervous?"

"No! Not at all. Not even a bit. Not even a fraction. Not a nth! Why, should I be?"

"You're rambling," he said.

"I'm sorry." She bit her lip. "I don't want you to think I'm seeking attention, or trying to emotionally blackmail you into feeling sorry for me."

"Sweetheart, we survived a horrific plane crash in which one of our friends died. We're intelligent beings, but we're only human. We're both suffering from grief and shock. After what happened in Vegas, it's natural that we'd gravitate toward each other for comfort. I don't think you're seeking attention. I'm worried about you. So tell me—why don't you feel like yourself?"

She blew out a long, shaky breath. "I've never felt like this before. I face everything head on. I know I said that when my relationship with Ian broke down, I ran away, but it didn't feel like that at the time. I felt as if I was taking steps to protect myself. I take action. It's what I do."

"But now?"

"I feel… powerless." It was such an insipid word to explain her sensation of utter futility. "I feel as if it doesn't matter what I do or say in this world; the earth is going to keep turning, and terrible things will happen even if I do my utmost to try to prevent them. I could stay at home all day and a plane could crash into my house. I feel terrified when I get into my car. I'm having bad dreams at night. I keep seeing Mike's face, his open eyes… and hearing the screams in the plane. Life is just shit, and there's nothing I can do about it..." She stopped, her chest heaving, hands shaking.

"All right," he said gently. "One thing at a time. First, I'm going to check you over, for real, okay?" When she nodded, he spent a few minutes taking her blood pressure, her temperature, and her pulse, and listening to her heart and lungs.

Afterward, he sat back in his chair. "Your blood pressure is a little high, but that's to be expected considering you feel stressed at the moment. I don't think you're ill, Roberta. What you're going through is perfectly normal."

"I don't care; I want it to stop."

"Well, we don't get to pick and choose our emotions," he said, firmly enough to remind her that he was a doctor and not just her friend. "They are what they are, and the best thing we can do is learn to deal with them. You admitted that you feel out of control, and you're obviously fighting that feeling. Maybe it would just be better to go with it."

"What do you mean?"

"Imagine you're in a rowing boat on the open sea. The wind's blowing up a gale. And you're standing in the boat, getting drenched, desperately trying to keep your balance and stop the boat rocking. But you're fighting against nature, and you're never going to win that way. The best thing you can do is to lie down in the boat and let the sea take you where it wants."

"It's not my natural way," she admitted.

"I know, and I'm not saying it's easy. But you can't force yourself to get over what you've been through. When the emotions come—and they will, for a long while yet—you have to ride them like waves and let them toss you about and sweep over you. You'll feel exhausted afterward, but the wave will have passed, and you pick yourself up and dry yourself off and start all over again. And eventually the waves will get smaller, and they won't have the strength to bowl you over like they did in the beginning."

It was a new concept for Roberta, and not one she was sure she could—or wanted—to attempt. And yet, what was the alternative? To carry on as she had been, in total panic at the thought that all her attempts at controlling her life were futile?

"What about the nightmares?" she asked him. "I don't often remember my dreams, but these are so vivid…"

"Usually they calm down as the memories of the traumatic event fade," he advised. "If you'd like, I can refer you to a therapist who could talk it all through with you."

"No, I don't want that." She'd gone to see a counsellor when she'd had all the trouble with Ian. She'd found the sessions awkward and embarrassing, unable to shake the feeling that the counsellor was judging her for the choices she'd made.

"I can give you sleeping pills," he said, "but I'd rather not. The best thing I can suggest at the moment is to get into a routine at night. Don't watch TV right before bed. Have a bath and a warm drink, and maybe record your thoughts somehow—write them down, or paint a picture, as you're very visual. Express how you're feeling before you turn the lights out."

"I'll try," she said.

"You need to take care of yourself," he said. "Don't push yourself too hard over the next few weeks."

"Okay."

He pursed his lips. "Hot sex before bed is also supposed to help."

Her eyebrows rose. "Loose tongue again?"

"Nope. I meant to say that." He smiled, got to his feet, and pulled her up. Then he wrapped his arms around her. "I'm sorry."

"For what?" she said, her voice muffled as she pressed her face into his shirt.

"For making your life harder at the moment. I don't regret the sex, but I do regret that. I wish it were simpler, and we could just date normally."

"Why can't we?" she asked, hating the note of pleading that had crept into her voice.

"I just can't." He kissed her hair. "Not right now. I'm sorry."

He wasn't going to explain. She clenched her hands in his shirt, feeling a surge of frustration. He knew what she'd been through with Ian. Couldn't he see how this was so hard for her? Secrets and lies… She hated them, and wished he'd just say 'I can't have a relationship now because I had a bad breakup and need time to recover,' or 'my mum left me and I don't trust women,' or whatever the big deal was that was keeping them apart.

Was there someone else? It was the most obvious reason for his hesitation. He'd never been linked with another girl and her gut feeling told her that wasn't the issue here. But could she be certain? Her instincts hadn't been great in the past.

Seeing him was the worst thing she could do. It wasn't doing her self-respect any good, and while she was involved with him in any capacity she would never find anyone else.

But there was something about this guy that got to her, as if, every time she looked at him, the fat baby with the bow fired an arrow right into her heart. Where his hands touched her, she burned. Her pulse doubled its rate whenever he walked into the room. And whatever Angus's reasons for trying to remain distant from her, he couldn't keep away from her any more than she could keep away from him. Every time he looked at her, the warmth in his eyes told her he liked her. And he'd said *I just can't… Not right now.* Did that mean there would come a time when he might want a relationship?

She could demand to know what he was hiding, but she had a feeling he wouldn't tell her, and that would only make things awkward between them. If she had any self-respect, she should toss her hair and tell him that if he wouldn't open up to her, she was done. But she didn't want to lose this. His friendship. His warm arms around her.

"Can I pick you up from work?" he said. "Take you back to my place?"

She moved back a little and looked up at him, confused. "You said you wished you could date normally."

"I know…"

"So it wouldn't be a date, then?"

"Do we have to give it a name? I want you, Roberta. I want you in my life, in my arms, in my bed. Does it have to be more than that?"

I deserve more than that, she thought to herself. But she wanted him too much.

"Okay," she whispered.

"I'll pick you up at five-thirty."

She nodded and collected her purse.

"Think about what I said," he told her. "About going with the flow."

Was he referring to the PTSD? Or to their relationship? Was he trying to tell her to go along with him until he was ready to commit?

"All right." She opened the door. "See you later." She slipped out and walked away, head down, her mind a whirl of thoughts and emotions.

Chapter Fifteen

It was close to six o'clock by the time Angus finally pulled up outside Bay of Islands Brides. It was raining, and he parked just down from the shop, the car lights showing the rain as yellow nails in the gathering gloom.

Half of him expected Roberta to have gone home. He'd seen the wariness in her eyes when she'd asked why they couldn't have a normal relationship, and he'd replied *I just can't*. He'd felt like a complete heel, because after what she'd been through she deserved so much more. He should have dealt with her medical query, given her a prescription, then sent her on her way.

Instead, he was sitting outside her place of work, hoping desperately that she hadn't gone home, planning to take her back to his house to do wicked things to her.

There was no hope for him. None at all.

The lights were out in both the bridal shop and the café. His heart sank. She'd got bored of waiting for him, and she'd gone home.

Fuck.

He was just about to start the engine again when he saw a flash of movement through the café window. His heart leapt. He watched Roberta exit the café, lock up behind her, and then run over to his car, holding her purse over her head to shield her from the rain.

She yanked open the passenger door and promptly fell inside, scattering raindrops over him. After closing the door, she looked across. Her skin glistened and her eyes glittered in the light of the street lamp overhead.

"Hello," she said.

"Hello."

"What are you smiling at? I look horrendous."

He cupped her cheek and kissed her.

"Oh," she said when he eventually drew back. "Not that horrendous then?"

He started the engine. "As ghastly as Medusa on a bad hair day." Smiling, he eased the car into the traffic.

"I've never been to your house," she said as they left the shops and bars behind and took the flyover out of town. "I bet it's terribly neat, with all the jars in rows and T-shirts folded neatly in the drawer."

"You think I have OCD?" he asked with some amusement.

"You strike me as a tidy kind of guy. Either that or it's a right mess because you work too hard to spend time on it."

He laughed, happy to have her with him. Even though she'd professed she was going through a difficult time earlier, she still lit him up like a light bulb.

"Somewhere in the middle," he said. "I confess I have a cleaner come in once a week. I try to keep tidy, but I hate vacuuming."

"Tell me about it. I have two cats."

"Crazy cat lady," he said, and smiled.

"Damn straight. Cats are better than men."

"Everything's better than men," he said, meaning it.

She chuckled and looked out into the dark night. "We are crazy," she whispered. "Aren't we? Seeing each other like this."

"Oh yeah. Certifiable." He navigated the roundabout and headed past Rafe and Phoebe's house. "It's your fault. You've bewitched me."

"Yep. Eye of newt, toe of… whatever."

"Wow. Shakespeare's rolling in his grave somewhere."

She wrinkled her nose. He held out his hand, and she slid hers into it.

"No Emily tonight then?" he asked, referring to Dominic's daughter. She often looked after her while Dominic did his rounds in town.

"No, I only have her once a week now, so Dominic and Fliss can have a night out. Fliss picks her up from school."

"Do you miss her?" He knew she had a soft spot for her niece.

"Yes. The house is quiet without her. And it was fun to work my way through the Disney movies. But I'm glad she gets on so well with Fliss."

"How's Fliss's new job going?"

"Good," she said. "I'm not surprised the college bit her hand off when she suggested holding acting lessons up here. It's a long way to

Whangarei, and it means not all of our youngsters are leaving the area for the cities."

He nodded, turning onto Kapiro Road. The rain beat down on the windscreen, the car's headlights casting two golden beams on the silvery road. Glancing down, he saw that Roberta's hands were clenched in her lap, her knuckles white. He slowed the car a little.

"You look nice today," he said, trying to take her mind off the journey. She'd unzipped her rain jacket, revealing a white cotton shirt beneath a stone-colored sweater. No knee-length boots today, but her black jeans flared over black ankle boots. He loved the way she dressed. She wasn't girly pink-and-white like her sisters, who were fond of glitter and sequins and sparkly clips in their hair, nor was she like the beautiful Fliss, who flaunted her designer labels. Roberta liked neutral colors and sleek cuts, and her makeup always looked natural. Tonight, she'd twisted her hair up in a messy bun, and untidy strands tumbled around her face. He wanted to kiss her until he filled her dreams with memories of their lovemaking, and all her fears evaporated like mist in the sunshine.

Slowing, he turned onto the gravel drive. Six letterboxes sat on the side of the road, and he passed the entrances to the other five houses, laying behind orchards of kiwifruit and mandarins, invisible in the darkness. His was the one at the end, and he slid the car through the trees and parked outside the house.

They got out of the car and ran across to the front door, and he unlocked it and let her pass him. After flicking on the switch that illuminated the small lamps around the walls of the living room, he tossed his keys onto the table and hung his jacket on the peg by the door.

"Oh Angus, this is lovely." She took off her boots, then stepped down into the living room. Conscious of the cool temperature, he turned on the gas fire, sending the flame leaping over the fake logs. What did it look like through her eyes? Tidy enough. A little sterile, maybe. A comfortable black sofa and chairs, a functional coffee table. His PlayStation. Not a lot of personal stuff, but then he spent hardly any time there.

"What's the garden like?" She went over to the window and pressed her nose against the glass.

"There's a lawn and some palm trees. No veggie patch. I don't get out there much, to be honest."

"Shame." She turned back to the room. "I love my garden. There's something about tending the plants that warms the soul."

"I feel the same way about humans."

She smiled. "Is that how you think about your patients? As plants that need to be tended?"

"Kinda, yeah. Most respond to careful nurturing. Occasionally you have to pull out a weed by the roots."

She laughed and walked over to the painting on the wall, the one colorful thing in the room. It depicted a young African woman with braided hair, wearing an elaborate beaded collar and headband. "She's beautiful," Roberta said.

"Her name is Farashuu," he told her. "It means butterfly."

"You know her?"

"Yes. I treated her and her mother in Kenya. Her mother, Hashiki, painted this to say thank you for healing them both."

Roberta turned to him with wide eyes. "You worked in Kenya?"

"I worked in lots of countries. She tried to teach me Swahili."

"Can you remember any of it?"

He pursed his lips. "*Wewe ni mrefu sana.* It means 'You are very tall.'"

She smiled. "When did you work there?"

He indicated with his head for her to follow him into the kitchen, turning lights on as he went. "I worked in the UK for two years after I graduated medical school here. Then I joined *Médecins Sans Frontières*—Doctors Without Borders. I came back to New Zealand about… three years ago now."

He opened the fridge. He hadn't really thought this through. What could he do her for dinner that wouldn't take forever but wouldn't make him look an idiot? "You're not vegetarian, are you?" he asked. "I've got some chorizo sausage and peppers. And potatoes and eggs. How about a kind of Spanish omelet?"

When she didn't reply, he glanced over at her to see her leaning on the kitchen counter, watching him.

"What?" he said.

She shook her head. "Just thinking about how I know so little about you. I mean, I knew you'd worked in the UK, but that was it."

"I don't talk about it much," he said.

"Why?"

He turned back to the fridge. As she hadn't dismissed the Spanish omelet idea, he started getting out the ingredients. "Just don't like discussing it."

"You're a very private person, aren't you?" she said softly.

He closed the fridge door and pulled a knife out of the block. "I guess."

"Is it me? Or are you like this with everyone?"

"It's not you," he said, sending her a wry smile before he began chopping the peppers.

She looked down at her hands, and he felt a twinge of guilt. He was asking her to share his bed; it wasn't fair to treat her like everyone else.

"What would you like to know?" he asked, a little warily.

Looking up again, she met his eyes, hers filled with such obvious pleasure that it warmed him through. "What countries did you work in?" she asked.

"All over Europe." He began to slice an onion. "France for over a year. I learned to speak French, which helped when we went to Africa—Kenya, Ethiopia, and Somalia. After that, we came back to Europe and went to Serbia, Ukraine, and Belarus." It took effort for him to say the word while keeping any inflection out of his voice. Move on, he told himself. "I loved every minute of it. I really felt as if I was doing some good, you know?"

He scooped the sliced onion and pepper into a bowl, then started on the potatoes.

"*We* came back to Europe?" Roberta said.

He paused for a moment, the knife blade resting on the potato. He hadn't even realized he'd said it.

Was he going to keep everything from her? Maybe if he told her a little about his life, she wouldn't feel so shut out.

He wanted to share, he realized. He wanted to let her in.

He sliced the potato smoothly. "My brother and I."

"Oh! You have a brother?"

"Had." He cleared his throat. "He died."

Her mouth formed an O for a moment. "I'm sorry, Angus."

He sighed and started on another potato. "My dad is a Kiwi, but my mother is Scottish. It's one reason we went to the UK—we met a lot of our family there, aunts and uncles, cousins."

"What was your brother's name?"

"Jamie."

"Older or younger?"

"He was about eighteen months older than me." He poured some oil into the frying pan and turned on the hob. "We'd never been to Scotland and had always wanted to go. He was a doctor too, so once I'd graduated, we went together. We stayed together and worked together wherever we went. We were very close."

It still hurt to talk about him. He tossed the potato into the pan and started frying it, wondering when the pain and anger would eventually subside.

"How did he die?" she asked from behind him.

"He had hypertrophic cardiomyopathy. It's a condition where the walls of the heart thicken causing a too-rapid heartbeat. He wasn't even aware he had it."

"Oh jeez, how awful. Did he die abroad?"

"No. We'd come home for a while. We'd been in New Zealand about four months, in Auckland. We were playing a game of rugby, and he just dropped to the floor. He was dead before the ambulance got there."

She circled the kitchen counter, slid her arms around his waist, and hugged him. "I'm so, so sorry. Thank you for telling me."

He put his free arm around her, squeezed her, and kissed her hair. "I don't talk about it much because it's too painful. But I'm glad you know." He gestured to the vegetables. "Come on then, pass me those. I haven't eaten since midday and I'm ravenous."

Chapter Sixteen

Once he'd finished the omelet, they served it up onto two plates with a side salad and carried it through to the living room.

Roberta curled up on the sofa and ate forkfuls of the hot omelet, watching the flames leaping in the gas fire. Her mind was spinning from what Angus had told her about his brother and his past. It was so odd to finally discover something about him. He'd obviously taken Jamie's death hard. For the first time, he seemed like a fully rounded person to her, and not just a cardboard cutout of someone for whom she had these inexplicable feelings. She'd known he must be warm-hearted to be a doctor, and she'd seen him in action on the plane. But learning about his time with Doctors Without Borders gave her a deeper understanding of how much he enjoyed helping people, and how much he wanted to do good.

"Is what happened to Jamie the reason why you decided to become a GP here in New Zealand?" she asked him.

He sat at the other end of the sofa, legs stretched out, tucking into his meal the way guys do, with bites three times the size of hers. He nodded. "We worked as a team. It would have felt odd going back to Europe without him by my side." He considered his plate for a moment, then continued eating.

She thought she could imagine how he must have idolized his older brother. She would never admit to idolizing Dominic and certainly not the irrepressible Elliot, but she admired them and respected them both, and she knew losing either of them would hit her hard.

"So did your Dad come from up here?" she asked, keen to take away his sadness, although she didn't really want to change the subject as she was enjoying finding out more about him.

"Nope. Aucklander. But we holidayed a lot in the Bay of Islands, and sometimes over on the Hokianga. After Jamie died, I knew I wanted to settle down somewhere in a smaller community. And a position came up at the Kerikeri surgery, so here I am." He smiled.

"Are your parents still alive?"

"Yep. Still in Auckland."

"Do you visit them a lot?"

He dropped his gaze to his plate and pushed the last few mouthfuls around with a fork. "Most weekends."

Roberta wasn't dumb. She knew there was something he hadn't told her about his family. But he'd finally opened up to her, so she wasn't going to push it. He obviously had his reasons for keeping things close to his chest, and she felt that the admissions he'd made were a sign that he was interested in getting to know her better.

It was strange to think they were married. She tried not to dwell on it, because they were just words; they didn't mean anything. But it was impossible to banish it completely from her mind when he was sitting there looking gorgeous. She glanced at her left hand, imagining what it would look like with a ring there catching the light on her third finger. He'd told her it was a terrible mistake, and yet as far as she knew he'd made no move to get the marriage annulled or to start divorce proceedings. And they'd now had sex twice. Maybe he was having second thoughts?

Placing his plate on the table, he lifted the bottle of wine and offered it to her. "Another glass?"

"What about you?" she asked, conscious that he'd only had water.

"Not if I'm driving you home afterward," he said. His gaze rested on hers, a touch mischievous. "Unless… you'd like to stay the night?"

She held her breath, her heart thumping. "Are you sure?"

"It would be nice to take our time for once, don't you think?"

This was crazy; no way should she say yes and get any deeper into this relationship until Angus had come clean with her, and she was as sure as a person could be that there were no secrets between them.

But his blue eyes were mesmerizing, and she couldn't look away. Her cats would be fine for one night on their own. She gave a small nod, and his lips curved up.

Without saying anything more, he got up and retrieved a second wine glass, topped them both up, and then held his up to her as if in a toast. She clinked hers against his, and they settled back to sip the rich, fruity wine.

"Mind you, I don't have a change of clothes or anything," she realized.

"That doesn't sound like the Roberta I know," he scoffed. "Bound by societal norms."

"What are you implying?"

He grinned. "You don't strike me as the sort of girl to pass up the opportunity of some great sex just because you don't have a change of panties."

"Great sex," she repeated softly. "Someone's very sure of themselves."

"I'm very sure of you, Ms. Goldsmith. Sex with you couldn't possibly be average."

The compliment warmed her, so she decided not to point out that she was actually Mrs. McGregor.

"I'll take you home tomorrow, first thing," he told her. "I promise."

"Okay." She turned on the seat so she could tuck her feet under his thigh.

"Tell me more about you," he said. "I want to know more."

So while the fire leapt and the rain began to lash at the windows, Roberta gradually peeled back the layers of her past and bared her soul, something she'd never thought she'd do again after she broke up with Ian. Angus asked her about her childhood, her school years, and what her brothers and sisters were like as she grew up. They spoke about the death of her father, and about Mike, and talked about grief for a while in a way she hadn't done before with anyone. Angus had all the practical advice of his profession, but he was also open about the feelings of loss and betrayal that the death of his brother had stirred up in him. For the first time, Roberta felt able to admit how shocked she'd been when she'd received the phone call about her father's heart attack, and also how difficult it had been to help her sister, Phoebe, who'd blamed herself for not being there when he died.

They talked until the rain stopped, and then she made him go outside with her, sliding open the doors to the garden so they could step out onto the deck, the light from the fire inside spilling out around them like melted butter.

"I just love gardens after it's rained," she said, breathing in deeply the smell of wet earth. "It makes me feel… alive. You can almost hear the leaves taking in the water and the grass growing."

He stood behind her and slid his arms around her waist. "I know what you mean. I think."

"Do you believe in God, Angus?"

"I'm not sure. Do you?"

"I'm not sure either. Don't worry about offending me."

He kissed her shoulder. "I've been with several patients as they've passed away. It's easy to think it's all electric pulses, but I've always had a sense of something more going on. I think we probably don't have the capacity to understand it yet."

"Einstein said that matter and energy are the same thing, didn't he? And it's impossible to destroy energy. So it seems obvious to me that whatever drives us goes on to be the lifeforce in other things—trees, plants, flowers. Even people. I think that's what reincarnation is, and déjà vu. It's our atoms going on to form other living things."

"It's a lovely idea."

"I like to think Dad is still with me in some way," she said. "Do you ever feel that Jamie's around you?"

She felt him breathe in, then exhale slowly. "Sometimes. It's hard to know if that's just wishful thinking, though."

"If I died, I wouldn't leave my loved ones. Have you ever read Daphne du Maurier's *The Loving Spirit*?"

"No. Isn't that an Emily Bronte poem?"

"Yes, that's where she got the title. It's a lovely story about a family through the generations. They build a ship named after the mother, and it's as if her spirit remains in the ship with her children and grandchildren. That's what I'd do. I'd never leave my family."

"You'd be a wonderful mother."

It was such a lovely thing to say that it made her eyes sting. Angus turned her in his arms and took her face in his hands. He obviously saw her glassy eyes, but he just smiled and lowered his lips to hers.

Roberta closed her eyes and lifted her arms around his neck. She was crazy about this guy, and her feelings weren't going away anytime soon. And he obviously felt something for her, too. She wasn't imagining this, was she? She couldn't imagine the way he was tightening his arms around her, the heat in his kiss, the low murmur of pleasure deep in his throat?

Before tonight, she might have said it was all physical, because it had been as if their desire had taken them over and left them little choice except to exorcise it by sleeping together. But tonight? They'd shared their hearts and minds, not their bodies, and she was convinced he wasn't untouched by that.

But now she wanted more, and as she slid her hands into his hair, she whispered, "I want you," against his lips.

"I want you too," he murmured, and moved back through the sliding doors into the living room, taking her with him. After pulling the doors shut, he cupped her face and kissed her again before saying, "Here, by the fire? Or do you want to go to bed?"

"Here."

He nodded and led her forward so they were standing in front of the sofa. He moved the coffee table to the side so the heat from the fire could reach them. Then he began to kiss her again.

Roberta sighed as he unzipped her jeans and helped her out of them. He pulled her sweater over her head and dropped it onto the chair, then unbuttoned her shirt. Easing it off her shoulders, he then pushed it down her arms and tossed that aside, too.

Leaving her in her underwear, he moved her to the sofa and gave her a gentle push. She fell backward onto the cushions, laughing, and he stood before her, smiling as he unbuttoned his jeans.

She began to sing *The Stripper*, and Angus grinned and slowed his movements, teasing her as he undressed. She watched him reveal his body gradually, enjoying the glimpses of tanned skin and defined muscle, turned on by the differences between them, his height, the breadth of his shoulders, the obvious difference in strength. Attraction occurred on so many levels, she thought as, clad in his boxers, he sank to his knees before her. Women had to be turned on mentally, but the physical was important too, and just the look of his hard biceps and powerful thighs was enough to give her an ache deep inside.

Leaning forward, he kissed her, pressing her onto her back on the sofa, and she stretched out, purring with pleasure at the feel of his warm hands on her skin. He unpopped the catch of her bra and drew it down her arms, then filled his palms with her breasts, kissing down her neck to take a nipple in his mouth.

Roberta arched her back and let out a long moan at the sensation of his tongue on the sensitive skin. He swapped to the other nipple, sucking until it was hard and extended, then started to kiss down over her stomach. Hooking his fingers in the elastic of her panties, he slipped them off, pushed her knees apart, and kissed over her hips and around her thighs.

She found herself holding her breath as he trailed his lips slowly down the crease of her thigh. Lifting her arms, she covered her eyes, shutting out the rest of the world, wanting to concentrate on the feeling of his warm breath on her skin. He brushed his thumb lightly up through her folds and pressed both hands to her thighs, parting her, opening her to his gaze. She bit her lip, stifling a moan as he blew warm air on her.

When he touched the tip of his tongue finally to her clit, she jerked and moaned. He chuckled and stroked a hand on her thigh before sliding his tongue deep into the heart of her.

Ohhh… the bliss of having a guy go down on you… It turned her molten inside, the lava flowing through her veins, bringing heat to her face and making her body burn. He licked and sucked, drawing out the pleasure for her, and when she slid a hand into his hair, he moved her fingers up to her breast. She kept her eyes closed and teased her soft nipples until they were hard, knowing he was watching her, and when the orgasm came, she clenched around his fingers, his murmurs of encouragement adding to her pleasure.

When she'd done, he gave her a gentle kiss between her legs, then pressed his lips up her body until he could kiss her properly.

"You taste amazing," he whispered against her lips. "Like crème caramel. So sweet."

"Mmm." She wrapped her arms around his neck. "That was yummy."

Reaching across to the coffee table that was just in reach, he retrieved his wallet, took out a condom, and lifted up long enough to divest himself of his boxers and roll the condom on. Then he lowered down and kissed her again.

"I've thought about this all day," he said, nuzzling her neck and touching his tongue to her skin. "I'm glad you came around this afternoon."

"So am I." She'd been worried that he'd be frustrated or exasperated at her making an appointment, but she'd wanted to see him because she trusted him more than anyone. It was an odd realization. Was it because they'd had sex? Or because of the experience they'd shared on the plane? Or did it go deeper than that?

No, she couldn't be in love with him. Surely. This was only the third time they'd slept together if she didn't count Vegas, and they hadn't even been dating before their marriage.

And yet, she'd known him for two years. She'd always had a thing for him, right from the beginning. And it was clear to her that what she felt for him was more than affection.

But oh dear, falling in love was a terrible idea right now, when she wasn't even sure whether he'd want to see her again. After Ian, she taken the broken pieces of her heart, stuck them together as best as she could, and locked it behind steel bars. And she had to make sure the lock remained untouched, because she had the feeling that if she let Dr. Angus McGregor get his hands on her heart and it ended up being broken a second time, there wouldn't be enough Super Glue in the world to put it back together again.

Chapter Seventeen

Angus moved her legs up around his hips, positioned the tip of his erection at her entrance, and then pushed forward. Her body welcomed him in, and he felt her warm, slick walls close around him, gripping him tightly as if they never wanted to let him go.

Her wide eyes stared into his, shining a dark green in the firelight. They were like an aquarium, he thought, her thoughts the fish swimming through the shining water. He wanted to ask her what she was thinking, but a frown marred her brow and he wasn't sure if he'd like the answer. So he kissed her instead, teasing her tongue with his until she sighed and relaxed beneath him.

"Mmm, you feel good," he murmured, thrusting slowly inside her. It was the understatement of the year; at that moment, lying in front of the fire, with this beautiful woman wrapped around him, Angus couldn't think of anywhere in the world he'd rather be.

She didn't say anything, but she continued to look into his eyes. He kissed her, stroked up her body, and told her how beautiful she was, but still she continued to stare up at him, her eyes full of an emotion he couldn't quite catch.

Eventually, he stopped moving, kissed her lips, and said, "Are you okay?"

She nodded.

"Tell me," he said, kissing her cheek, her nose, and back to her mouth.

She sucked her bottom lip for a moment as if debating whether to tell him. Then eventually she whispered, "I'm worried I'm falling in love with you."

He felt a twist inside him, and he frowned. "Oh, sweetheart."

"I'm sorry," she said hurriedly. "I didn't mean it. Just forget I said anything."

"It's okay." He kissed her. "There would be something seriously wrong with us if we weren't a little in love by now."

"We?"

He began to move inside her again, and even though he knew he should be cursing himself for letting her fall for him, his heart was filled with joy. "I'm crazy about you, Bobcat. Can't you tell?"

Her eyes shining, she laughed at the nickname. "I didn't realize you knew I was called that when I was younger."

"Oh, I've been paying attention." He moved her legs higher, around his waist, and changed the angle of his hips so he was grinding against her. She gasped, and he smirked and thrust harder.

"Oh God," she gasped, digging her nails into his skin.

"Yes…" He kissed her hard, delving his tongue into her mouth, and she moaned and locked her ankles behind his back. He wasn't going to last long like this.

To his relief, he felt her muscles clenching around him, and then she was coming, saying his name over and over again, "Angus, Angus… oh Angus…" Her face was creased with pleasure, her throaty sighs such a turn on that he felt his own climax build and then it hit him. All the muscles in his groin tightened, and heat rushed up from his balls and burst from him in seven or eight clenches so powerful he thought he lost consciousness for a moment.

When he finally opened his eyes, Roberta's cool green ones were watching him. Her face was flushed, and a small smile played on her lips.

"Mmm," she said. "Wow, now I'm knackered."

He laughed and withdrew, disposed of the condom, and then collapsed onto the sofa, pulling her into his arms. "I could sleep for a week."

"Maybe we should," she murmured. "Just stay here like this and let the world go on without us."

He looked up at the ceiling, his smile fading as he remembered that he'd promised Katrina he'd go to Auckland that weekend. He brushed the thought away. *Being an ostrich again, Angus?* But he wasn't going to think about it now, with the fire hot on his skin, the night dark outside, Roberta in his arms, and hours yet before he had to let her go.

*

The rain continued through the night, but by the morning the storm had blown itself out, and Angus woke to sunlight streaming through the curtains. His phone told him it wasn't quite six a.m., so he had plenty of time yet before he had to get to work.

Behind him, Roberta was pressed up against his back, her knees tucked beneath his, her arms around his waist. Shifting on the bed, he turned over to look at her.

It had been a long while since he'd spent the night with someone. In his early twenties, he'd met a girl in France he'd been very fond of, but she'd made it clear she had no interest in leaving her home country, and he'd known all along that it had been a temporary agreement. Since then, he'd gone to bed with girls over the years, and had a few relationships along the way, but it had been ages since he'd felt like this about someone.

After they'd made love on the sofa, they'd retired to bed with the bottle of wine and a box of chocolates, and they'd cuddled up and watched a movie on his iPad, enjoying the coziness of being tucked up while the rain hammered down outside. He'd had a great evening, and he was disappointed it was over.

Her eyelids fluttered open, she blinked and focused on him, and then smiled. "Hey."

"Hey," he said.

"What's the time?"

"Just gone six."

"Oh, okay. What time do you want to leave?"

"Seven? Is that early enough for me to drop you off home?"

"That'll be great."

"So… we've got plenty of time…" He moved closer to her, sliding his arms around her and nuzzling her neck. She was all soft warm skin and interesting curves, and she still smelled of muffins.

"Mmm." She lifted her arms around his neck and raised her face for his kiss.

They made love slowly, their whole world the heated space beneath the duvet, thinking of nothing but each other's pleasure. He pulled her on top of him and let her ride him for a while, enjoying watching her as she rocked her hips, her chocolate-brown hair tumbling down her back. And then he lifted her off him, rolled her over, and pulled her back against his chest, sliding into her from behind. When her gasps and sighs turned to moans, he thrust them both to a climax, and he decided this was absolutely the best way to start a working day.

*

By seven, they were showered and dressed and in the car, heading for the town center, because she'd left her car in the car park behind the Brides shop. They stopped at the petrol station on the way to pick up a coffee and a muffin each, and then continued on past the fields.

It was still dark, the sky just beginning to lighten to a dull gray. Roberta looked down at where Angus held her hand as he drove. She felt as if she was radiating bliss, filled with the afterglow of pleasurable lovemaking.

"Thank you for a lovely evening," she said. "I'm tempted to suggest we play hooky and take the day off, but I have a feeling it isn't something the responsible Dr. McGregor would do."

"I wouldn't dream of it, Ms. Goldsmith," he said with a grin.

Her lips twitched. "Technically, I'm Mrs. McGregor," she said before she could think better of it.

Immediately, she regretted the words as his smile froze and he returned his gaze to the road, removing his hand from hers on the pretense of having a sip of his coffee.

"Angus," she said, her heart rate speeding up, "I'm teasing you. Come on, we've got to be able to laugh about it."

He smiled, although it didn't reach his eyes. "Yeah, you're right."

She wished she hadn't said anything, but now she had it seemed silly to pass up on the chance to sort things out. They'd both admitted last night that they were falling for each other. It made no sense to keep brushing the issue of the marriage certificate under the table.

"We do need to talk about it though," she pressed gently. "About what we're going to do."

He gave a small nod, although he didn't reply.

"I was thinking…" She nibbled her bottom lip. Should she say what had been on her mind? Oh, what the fuck… "Maybe… we shouldn't do anything."

He glanced at her. "What do you mean?"

She gave a shy shrug. "Perhaps we could see how things go. We seem to be getting on quite well…"

He replaced his coffee cup in the holder and returned his gaze to the road. "I'm sorry, but that's not an option."

Feeling as if he'd slapped her around the face, she swallowed and looked out of the window.

"I'm sorry," he said softly, "but it just isn't. It's out of my hands."

"I don't understand," she blurted out in frustration. "I know we'd never have gotten married if we were sober—we weren't even dating then, for Christ's sake. But now we're seeing each other and it's going really well…"

"We can't stay married," he said. "I'm really sorry; I know what you went through with Ian. You deserve so much more than I can give you. I've tried to keep away from you. I shouldn't have asked you to stay last night." He ran a hand through his hair.

Roberta was as much puzzled as she was frustrated. "Why can't you just tell me what the problem is?"

"Not everyone wants to reveal their soul," he said, his voice a tad sharp. "We're obviously attracted to each other, and maybe in the future there could be more between us, but for now I just can't make the commitment you want. I'm sorry."

Hurt and angry, she glared at him. "So what, then? I'm guessing we can't get an annulment now we've slept together?"

"There's no such thing in New Zealand anyway. A marriage can be deemed void by the courts but only if you're related to your partner or if you entered the marriage unwillingly."

"So what are the options then? We wait for a divorce?"

He hesitated. "I guess."

"How long does that take?"

"You have to have been separated for two years."

"Two years!" Roberta's jaw dropped. "We've got to wait two years before we can apply for a divorce?"

"I think it's a lot quicker in Nevada, but we'd have to move there." He glanced at her then, his eyes filled with regret. "I'm sorry."

"So you're not interested in making a go of it with me, but I've got to wait two years until I can marry anyone else?" Anger rose through her, at both him and at herself for getting into this situation. "Jesus, I've been so stupid."

"Roberta…"

"Don't," she snapped. "I'm not blaming you because it was my fault too that we're in this situation. And of course you'd take the sex if it was handed to you on a plate."

"It's not like that," he said.

"Oh, isn't it?"

"I told you last night that I'm falling for you too. That I'm crazy about you."

"They're just words, Angus. Useless words. What we did in Vegas was a stupid mistake. But if you had no interest in exploring the idea of a relationship with me, you shouldn't have slept with me again; you shouldn't have encouraged me."

"I know." The muscles bunched at the corner of his jaw. "I'm sorry."

"Will you stop saying you're sorry?"

"I don't know what else to say." He indicated around the roundabout, then slowed to pull into the car park.

"You're really not going to explain?" She was almost speechless with incredulity.

He stopped and put the handbrake on, but left the car running. "I can't. And I am sorry for that."

"I can't believe you!" She gathered up her purse and the paper bag with the muffin, then picked up her coffee. The lid came off and some slopped onto her hand, and she jammed the lid back on crossly. "I can't believe men! And I can't believe me! Why am I so fucking stupid?"

"Roberta…"

She opened the door, got out, and walked off to her car, leaving him to sort out closing his car door behind her. Her hands were shaking as she opened it, but she finally did it. She got in, started the engine, and drove off without giving him another glance.

It was only a short drive home, but she steamed all the way. When she got there, she went inside, hung up her jacket, and stood in the living room, looking out at her garden.

There was no sign of Jasmine or Rosie, both cats probably out and about, catching the early morning sun. She was alone again. Naturally.

All of a sudden, her anger drained away, and she lowered onto the sofa dispiritedly. She wasn't going to cry, she told herself. She was better off without him.

Her eyes were only stinging because there were onions somewhere in the house.

SERENITY WOODS

Chapter Eighteen

Roberta decided she was done with men. You couldn't trust them, and all they did was make you miserable. She didn't need one. She already had one niece; soon the rest of her siblings would start having kids, and she'd be the best auntie it was possible to be. She didn't need a man at home; she was perfectly capable of unscrewing jars and removing spiders by herself. And as for sex… that was what vibrators were for, and a vibrator didn't argue back.

She wasn't going to let herself be as upset as she had been with Ian. That had nearly destroyed her, and she couldn't bear to go down that road again. She might have admitted to Angus that she was falling in love with him, but hopefully she'd nipped that in the bud before it turned into an emotional form of a weed capable of engulfing half the garden.

It was easy to distract herself during the day, with the café as busy as ever, her family popping in and out of the shop, and running other errands like picking up Emily when Fliss was busy with a class at the college.

It was easy when she got home, went into the garden, and spent the few hours until it grew dark tending her vegetable patch, turning over the rich earth, sowing some seeds and putting others in trays inside to protect them from any frosts.

It was easy while she was cooking her dinner, dishing it up, and eating it, watching one of her favorite shows on TV.

It wasn't so easy once she'd washed up, it was dark, and it was just her and Rosie and Jasmine for the rest of the evening.

She painted some of the picture she was working on—a portrait of Emily in her ballet dress for Dominic's upcoming birthday in August. It was coming along quite well, and she spent a few hours each night adding depth to the colors and filling in some of the background. But it just reminded her of the painting on Angus's wall and the way they'd made love on the sofa in front of the fire.

She worked on a bullet journal she'd started recently, filling in the dotted pages with doodles and notes, but it was impossible to stop her mind wandering. In the end, she placed the journal aside and lay on the sofa, listening to music and drinking wine, while the wintry wind blew rain onto the windows, and Jasmine and Rosie curled up at her feet.

Could she spend a lifetime alone like this? She lay in the semi-darkness, the jazz music spiraling around her, and felt a deep sadness creep over her. She understood why some people made the decision to remain single. It was nice to be selfish, and not to have to worry about someone else's needs or wants. Not to have to compromise or put your own wishes and dreams aside because they didn't fit in with your partner's. She could watch what she wanted on the TV, or take a holiday whenever and wherever she felt like it. She didn't have to put up with anyone else's moods or demands.

But deep down, she wanted more than that out of life. Why couldn't things have been different between her and Angus? For the first time, she let herself think about what it might have been like if they'd gotten married for real, shared a bed, a home, had children… How would it feel to have the man you love come inside you without the barrier of a condom, and know that at that moment you could be making a baby, a whole other person? What incredible magic that was!

She'd thought about having children before, but it was the first real time she'd pictured herself pregnant, giving birth, holding a baby in her arms. The answering tug of need inside her took her breath away. Was this broodiness? This unusual, wistful yearning?

She could tell herself she was happy until the cows came home, but Roberta had always tried to be honest with herself. And the truth was that she did want those things. A partner—no, a husband, a real one, a man who'd committed himself to her not with a certificate that meant nothing after a drunk night, but one who'd stood beside her at the altar and promised before God and their family and friends to love her for the rest of their lives, forsaking all others. A man who desired her, who needed her, and who wanted to make a family with her, and be at her side as they had their children and brought them up together. She wanted a baby she could love and cherish, a tiny baby boy or a little girl in whom she could instill her values, teaching them the things that were important to her.

It was what most women wanted, and most women got, one way or another. Was she not entitled to these things, too?

But it was so hard to put herself out there, to start a new relationship, and to learn to trust and love again, when she'd been hurt so badly. In the end, though, it was her decision. Either she kept her heart walled up and refuse to open up to another man. Or she accepted that she was going to have to kiss a few frogs before her prince turned up.

Her mind conjured up a picture of a frog turning into Angus with a crown on his short brown hair, and she gave a wistful smile. That was a fairytale ending unlikely to come true. Why wasn't he interested in having a relationship with her? Why was he working so hard to keep himself distant?

There were too many questions and not enough answers, and Roberta eventually went to bed, curling up with her cats. It was Saturday tomorrow, she thought, and it promised to be a good day, because the girls were coming around in the evening. She'd spend the day making cakes and thinking of some games they could play. It would be Libby's first evening out since Mike died, and although she was by no means expecting Libby to forget what had happened, it would be nice to see her smile, and remind her that they were all there for her.

Would any of them ask her what was going on between her and Angus? She wasn't sure if any of them had noticed. Hopefully, she could keep it a secret, and use the evening as a distraction from the ever-present image of Angus in her mind.

*

Cathy and Angie were covering her in the café on Saturday morning for one of her rare days off. So she had a lie in and a leisurely bath, then went into the kitchen, put on her apron, and took out her big folder of recipes.

First, she made a batch of tiny spinach-and-cream-cheese muffins, then another batch of cheese-and-bacon ones. She put the ingredients in her bread maker and set it to kneading the dough, then made some mini ham quiches that could be eaten in one bite. When the dough was done and had risen for the first time, she cut it into small rolls and set it aside to rise again, then set to making the sweet things—miniature chocolate eclairs, fairy cakes with buttercream frosting, and chocolate brownies cut into bite-sized pieces.

She was happiest while she was baking, and she hummed along to the music playing in the background, stopping only for a cup of tea, which she drank sitting out on the deck, curling up on the outdoor sofa under the cover and looking out at her veggie patches with pleasure.

She realized that something had happened last night. In accepting that she did want a family, it was as if she'd finally gotten up from the crossroads where she'd been sitting for years, taken a fork in the road, and set off on a new journey. She wasn't going to pretend any longer that she would be happy growing old as a spinster with cats. It wasn't going to be easy, and she didn't expect the perfect guy to fall into her lap, but she'd made the decision, and it surprised her how much better it made her feel.

Pushing aside a twinge of disappointment that the guy in her future was unlikely to be Angus, she went back into the kitchen and continued with her baking.

Everything went fine until just after four, when there was a knock at the door.

She sighed. Someone was early. Maybe Dominic was dropping Fliss off or something. She put the hot tray of freshly baked rolls onto the table, wiped her hands on her apron, went to the door, and opened it.

It was Ian.

For a moment, she felt as if all the air had been sucked out of the room. She hadn't seen him for a whole year, since he'd come up to comfort her after the death of her father. And it had been six months since she'd spoken to him on the phone. She could still remember how she'd felt after that phone call, the way her feelings had tangled like a ball of wool when one of the cats got it. He'd spent ages telling her how much he missed her, only to let slip reluctantly that his wife was pregnant with their second child. Angry at having her emotions toyed with, she'd hung up on him, and he hadn't called since.

She should shut the door in his face, get back to her baking, and refuse to speak to him ever again.

He leaned against the doorjamb, his posture suggesting tiredness and unhappiness. "Robbie," he said, his nickname for her. The word came out as a long sigh of relief, sending a shiver right down her spine. "I've missed you."

She swallowed hard, self-consciously brushing a hand over the flour-dusted apron, the other hand touching her hair. "What are you doing here?"

"Can I come in?"

"I've got people coming around in a couple of hours. I'm baking."

"It smells amazing. I won't keep you long, I swear. I just need to talk to you."

She chewed her bottom lip, not sure what to do. But he'd come all the way from Christchurch, maybe even driven up from Auckland, judging by his tired posture, so she knew he must have a good reason for wanting to see her.

And she had to admit, it was good to see him, too. She'd loved this man for five years before they'd finally parted ways. It was impossible to eradicate every ounce of feeling she had for him.

Reluctantly, she stepped back and let him in, closing the door behind him.

"I like this house," he said. "It surprises me that you're living in the middle of nowhere though. You're such a city girl."

"I was." She walked past him into the kitchen, switched the coffee machine on, and set about making them both a cup. "Not anymore."

"Are you on your own still?"

"I have my cats." She caught the curve of his lips and threw him a wry glare. "Don't even go there."

"I wouldn't dream of it." He perched on a stool, bending to sniff the muffins on the plates. "These smell fantastic."

She watched the hot coffee fill the cup. "You can have *one*. They're for my friends."

He took one, popped it into his mouth, and sighed as he chewed. "I haven't eaten since this morning."

She passed him the full cup and started on her own. "You came up from Auckland?"

"Yeah. And there were roadworks at Wellsford. Took fucking forever."

"I always feel it's a longer journey than it should be. I haven't been back to Auckland since I left." Removing her cup, she gestured with her head for him to follow her, walked into the living room, and out onto the deck. She sat on one of the comfy chairs, and Ian took the other. There was about another hour until sunset, and the dying sun had bled onto the garden, turning it a deep orange-red.

"Veggies?" he said with some amusement. "You're a gardener now?"

"I use them at the café," she replied, somewhat defensively. "Don't come into my house and make fun of me."

His smile faded. "I wasn't, I swear. I'm sorry. I'm just surprised. But it's amazing, what you've done here."

She sipped her coffee. She wasn't going to make this easy for him. He'd hurt her too badly, too often, for her to welcome him with open arms.

The chickens were coming home to roost, having a last peck around the hen house before they retired for the night. She watched a pair of rosellas swoop across the garden and alight on the fence at the end, their brilliant colors painting a rainbow on the wood.

"Robbie," he said, "don't be angry with me."

"I'm busy and I don't have long," she said, a little sharply. She felt tired, exhausted from carrying the weight of the past. She desperately wanted to move on and cut the chains of this relationship that were holding her back. If Ian hadn't been the way he was, maybe she'd have trusted Angus a bit, and not felt the need to press him into something he wasn't ready for. "What do you want?"

"You," he said simply. "I want you back."

Chapter Nineteen

Roberta stared at him. Her heartbeat sounded loud in her ears. "What?" she said.

He cleared his throat and leaned forward, his elbows on his knees, the coffee cup dangling in his fingers. "I'm sorry I haven't rung for a while. Things have been... difficult."

"Oh?"

"Yeah. Lyn lost the baby."

Roberta's brain was spinning, and it was difficult to breathe, despite the cool air wrapping around them. "I'm sorry to hear that," she said awkwardly.

His lips twisted. "You don't have to say that."

"I meant it. Of course I did. I wouldn't wish that on anyone. How far gone was she?"

"Four months." He ran a hand through his hair. "It was fucking horrific. I've never seen so much blood."

Roberta closed her eyes, inhaled, and blew it out slowly. "When did this happen?" she asked.

"Not long after we last spoke."

So, four or five months ago, then. *Things have been... difficult*, he'd said. She sipped her coffee, even though it was a struggle to swallow, waiting for him to elaborate.

"Things hadn't been good for us for a while," he said eventually. "And after that it got worse. She blamed me—said it was all the stress of everything that caused the miscarriage." His gaze flicked over to her before he lowered it to the ground again.

"She blamed me," Roberta said.

"She was angry, and in pain. It was easier to blame us than to think there was something wrong with the baby."

Roberta felt sick. "Why are you telling me this? I don't want to know all this."

"I'm sorry, she's wrong of course, it was nothing to do with you. I told her that. She hated me defending you. Things went from bad to worse. And I ended up moving out."

Her eyebrows rose. "You've left the house?"

"I've left Christchurch. I'm staying at your apartment in Auckland. I kept it, after you'd left. I suppose I always hoped you'd come back to me."

Roberta took a few deep breaths, determined to think clearly about this. "Did you leave, or did she throw you out?"

"I left," he said. He held her gaze, his eyes clear. "Do you believe me?"

She put her coffee cup on the table. "It doesn't matter whether I do or not. Your marriage has broken down, and now you're on your own and looking for company, and I'm the first number in your little black book."

"Don't do that," he said harshly. "Don't make out that you meant nothing to me. I loved you, you know that. I still love you. That's why I'm here."

She said nothing. He might be speaking the truth. But what did that actually mean? She'd accepted some time ago that it would have to be her who made the break, because Ian would always run to her if he didn't get the comfort and attention he needed from his wife. Was this more than that?

"I'm sorry it's taken me so long to sort things out," he said. "I'll understand if you don't want anything to do with me. But you know how I feel about you. You know I was devastated when you left. I wish I'd been stronger and walked out of the marriage then, but with the baby and everything… I put loyalty and duty first, and I shouldn't have done, because Lyn never loved me. And I never felt about her the way I feel about you."

Roberta rose and walked to the edge of the deck, looking out at the garden. She leaned against the post, resting her head on the wood. What was she to make of all this? Two years ago, she would've killed to have Ian say these things to her. And if he'd said it when he'd last visited her, when her father died, she'd have flung her arms around him and never let him go. But now?

"I know it's been hard for you," he said. "I'm not expecting anything. And I don't expect you to answer now. But I didn't want to tell you over the phone. I drove all the way up here. I'm crazy about you, Robbie, I always have been, and I always will be."

Angus had said something similar to her only days ago. Her stomach did a strange little flip when she remembered the moment, lying in bed, with him inside her. At the time it had filled her with joy, and she'd been convinced their future lay together. Then they'd argued, and the dream had shattered into a million pieces.

Still, she hadn't yet gotten to the point where her heart failed to leap when the phone rang. It wasn't over with Angus, no matter what she tried to tell herself.

She turned and shoved her hands into the pockets of her jeans, leaning on the post. "I've met someone else."

Ian's eyes widened. They studied each other for a long moment.

"I suppose I should have guessed you'd be snapped up," he said softly. "How fucking arrogant to think you'd wait for me."

She pushed a stone across the deck with her toe. "I'm not sure it's going to come to anything yet. It's very early days."

"Who is he?"

"He's a doctor. I've known him for a couple of years, since I came back up here. He was with me when the plane crashed."

Ian stared at her. "What plane?"

Christ, of course, he didn't know. "Did you read about the plane from LA that had to make a forced landing in Rarotonga?"

"You're kidding me? You were on that?"

She nodded. "One of my friends died in the crash, and his girlfriend was badly injured."

He rose, put down his cup, and came over to her. "I am so, so sorry." He put his arms around her.

She stood stiffly for a moment, then sighed and rested her cheek on his chest. "It was awful. It's been a horrible couple of weeks."

"I can imagine." He stroked her hair. "Are you okay? Were you injured?"

"No, not really. Not physically, anyway. Just… bad dreams, you know."

"You should have rung me. I can't believe it. I nearly lost you." His voice hitched and he buried his face in her hair.

Roberta sighed. He still used the same aftershave, the familiar scent taking her back to happier times. Wasn't this what she'd always longed for? For him to come to her and tell her he'd left his wife and he wanted to be with her? Angus didn't want her. It didn't matter what words he said—his actions told her he wasn't prepared to commit to her. She'd slept with him three times; she'd been in a relationship with Ian for five years. Surely, that had to mean something?

"Do you love him?" Ian asked hoarsely.

She cleared her throat and pulled back, and he let his arms drop. "It's too early for that."

"Are you sleeping with him?" he demanded. She just met his gaze, and he lowered his, his jaw knotting. "Sorry," he muttered.

"You can't do this," she said, somewhat desperately. "You can't just walk back into my life when you feel like it and act as if everything's all right." Anger blended with her frustration. "I waited for you for five years. Did you really think I'd still be sitting here when you chose another woman over me? You were good, but you weren't that good."

"I thought you were happy with the arrangement. You said you enjoyed the freedom and living on your own in the week."

"I was twenty years old! I didn't know what I wanted. I was in love with you, and I'd have said anything to keep you. You seduced me, knowing perfectly well I thought you were single at the time, and then kept me dangling with the promise of a future you had no intention of fulfilling. And now that your wife has finally thrown you out, you're panicking because you're on your own and you've come running back to me." Tears stung her eyes, and she dashed them away furiously.

"You're right that I shouldn't have slept with you when I was married," he whispered. "And I shouldn't have kept the affair going over five years. I'm weak, I know. But the only reason I couldn't break up with you was because I'm in love with you. I stayed with Lyn because of the baby and because I felt I should try to make it work, but the marriage fell apart because I never loved her like I love you. If only I'd met you first! Life would have been so different."

His face was filled with anguish, twisting her stomach into a knot.

"I wish you hadn't come here," she said, backing away from him, wiping her eyes with the heel of her hand. "I was just getting over you and moving on. Angus isn't perfect, but he has shown me that it's possible for me to find happiness with someone else."

"Is that it, then? Are we over?"

They stood there for a long time, watching each other. Roberta wanted to tell him to leave and never to contact her again, but her mouth wouldn't form the words. She'd loved him for so long, and missed him so much. He was as handsome as ever, his dark eyes still giving her all the shivers. Memories of the things they used to do in bed rose to the surface of her mind. If he truly had left his wife… If he really did want to be with her in a proper relationship…

"I don't know," she said, hating herself for the answer, but unable to turn her back on him, even now.

He let out a long breath. "That's not the worst answer you could have given."

"I'm not saying anything…"

"I know." He held up a hand. "Look, I've got to go back to Auckland tonight because I've got a meeting early tomorrow."

"On Sunday?"

"You know the restaurant business is twenty-four-seven." That was true; he'd very rarely taken a day off work. "But I could come back up on Monday," he said. "And we could talk some more."

"You can't stay here," she said immediately. That wouldn't work at all, even if he stayed in her spare room; the temptation would prove too much, and her willpower wasn't that strong.

"Of course. I'll book a motel room for the night." He reached out and cupped her cheek. "Don't look so relieved. I'm not just looking to get back in your bed, Robbie. I want to get back in your life, permanently. I've treated you like shit in the past, and I want to make it up to you. I want to put you on a pedestal and treat you like a queen for the rest of your days, I swear."

He brushed her cheek with his thumb. She closed her eyes for a moment, her heart filled with memories.

Angus.

Her eyes flew open, and she stepped back. "Don't," she said.

He lowered his hand. "I'd better go."

She followed him through to the front door. "Drive carefully."

"Yeah." He stepped out into the wintry evening, then stopped and turned to her. "So I'll come up Monday?"

She didn't know what to say, so she just said, "Okay," and he nodded and gave a relieved smile.

"I'll see you then." He leaned forward and kissed her cheek. Then he strode off to his car, and within a few minutes he was heading out onto the main road, the tail lights disappearing into the distance.

Roberta went in, shut the door, and walked through to the kitchen. Her head spun with thoughts and her heart whirled with emotions. But she had no time to think it through now. The girls would be arriving soon, and she still had a few things to do.

She wasn't going to think about him. She'd concentrate on her friends, and then tomorrow when she was on her own, she'd sit down with a pen and paper and make a list of everything. She wasn't going to make an emotional decision; she'd make sure she thought with her brain and not her heart.

So she plated up all the food, readied the wine glasses, changed into a comfy pair of gray pajamas with pink elephants all over them, tied up her hair in a messy bun, put on some music, and by the time Dominic dropped Fliss off at six, she was ready.

Fliss waved goodbye to her husband then came in carrying a bottle of wine and a box of chocolates. "Hey!"

"Hey!" Roberta hugged her. "Brought your PJs?"

"Of course! I didn't want to wear them in the car in case we were stopped by the police." Laughing, Fliss extracted a pair of gorgeous cream satin pajamas and gestured along the corridor. "I'll go get changed."

Ten minutes later, Bianca arrived with Karen, and then five minutes after that, Phoebe pulled up with Libby, who got out of the car, collected a pair of crutches from the back seat, and walked awkwardly over.

Roberta kissed her sister, then gave Libby a huge hug. "Hey, you."

"Hey." Libby squeezed her back, wobbling a bit on the crutches. "Thanks for inviting me."

"Of course! Wouldn't be the same without you." Roberta pulled back and looked her in the eye. "How are you doing? Shit?"

"Shit," Libby agreed. "I can't promise I'm going to be a lot of fun tonight. Are you sure you want me to stay?"

"There are tissues on the table," Roberta said. "I'm all prepared."

Libby gave a wry smile and handed over a bottle of wine. "I'll get changed into my PJs."

"This is such a good idea of yours," Bianca said, coming back into the living room in a pair of old blue cotton pajamas. "I feel like I'm fifteen all over again."

"We should play One Direction songs and try on each other's shoes," Phoebe said, and everyone laughed.

Roberta watched them bringing in the wine glasses and the plates of food, and felt a swell of emotion as they exclaimed about how lovely

119

it all was and praised her for her efforts. These were some of her favorite people in all the world, and she felt incredibly lucky to know them all. Jeez, she wished Ian hadn't chosen tonight of all nights to show up. She felt confused and unsettled, and she'd so been looking forward to the evening.

"Hey," Karen said, "I ran into Angus yesterday, and we chatted for a few minutes, and when I happened to mention your name, he blushed." She gave Roberta a mischievous look. "What's going on there?"

Everyone turned to look at her, their lips curving up at the thought of a bit of friendly gossip.

And Roberta burst into tears.

Chapter Twenty

"Oh, holy shit," Karen said, looking alarmed. "What did I say?"

"I'm sorry." Roberta pressed her fingers to her lips. "I've had a bad day. It's not you."

"Aw, come here." Phoebe led her to the sofa in front of the fire, and they all gathered around, Phoebe on her left, Bianca on her right, Libby and Karen in the armchairs, Fliss curling up on the floor. "Pour us all a wine, Fliss," Phoebe said. "I think we're going to need it."

"I'm so embarrassed," Roberta said with a short laugh, wiping her eyes. "I'm always the non-emotional one."

"You are," Bianca said, "so it must mean something that you're upset."

"Here." Fliss passed her a glass of sparkling wine.

"Thank you." She took a large swallow and rubbed a hand over her face. "I really am sorry. It's just that someone I wasn't expecting turned up only an hour ago and he made me all…" She waved her hand in the air.

"Angus?" Karen asked with a frown.

Roberta shook her head. "Ian."

Everyone's eyes widened, even Fliss's, so Roberta knew that Dominic must have told her what had happened with her ex.

"Fuck," Phoebe said. "Ian was here?"

Roberta nodded, blew out a long breath, and had another big swallow of wine.

"Screw the wine," Libby said, "someone get the vodka."

*

After everyone had gotten themselves the drink they fancied, they all listened as she paraphrased what Ian had told her. She didn't leave anything out, because what was the point? She was far too close to this, and she needed perspective. If anyone could help her sort out what to do, it was her sisters and closest friends.

"So he's really left his wife?" Phoebe chose a cream cheese mini muffin and popped it in her mouth. "Or did she throw him out?"

"He says he left."

"Do you believe him?" Libby asked.

Roberta hesitated. "Does it matter?"

Bianca tipped her head from side to side. "It would matter to me. Because if she threw him out, he wants you as a backup. If he walked out, it's because he realized he really does love you more than her, and he's finally made the break." They all nodded their agreement.

"I don't know," she said honestly. "He didn't look away when he told me. I think he was telling the truth. But I don't know if I'm telling myself that because it's what I want to believe."

"Is it what you want?" Karen asked. "Do you want him back?"

"I don't know. I miss him. A year ago, when Dad died, I'd have said yes, of course. Now? I'm not so sure."

"Why?" Fliss asked softly. "Is this because of Angus?"

"Oh, I forgot about that," Karen said. "He definitely blushed when I said your name."

"What's going on there?" Libby wanted to know. "Come on, spill the beans. I'm living vicariously through you now."

Roberta sent her a wry look. "There's not much to say…"

"There's heaps to say," Libby said firmly, "and I want all the dirty details."

"Jesus."

"I can't believe it," Bianca said, "are you really seeing him?"

Knowing they weren't going to let it go, Roberta gave in. "You know that night in Vegas when you all went off and Angus and I stayed behind?" When they all nodded, she continued, "Well, we woke up in Angus's room, semi-naked, handcuffed together, and… with a marriage certificate on the bed."

They all stared at her.

"What?" Phoebe said.

Roberta put her face in her hands.

"Holy fuck," Bianca said. "You're married?"

"It's nothing," Roberta said, her voice muffled, "it's just a piece of paper…" She sat back with a sigh. "Except of course it's not, because apparently you can't have a marriage annulled in New Zealand, so that means we've got to wait two years before we can apply for a divorce, and oh Jesus, your faces make me want to die, I'm so embarrassed."

"It's all right," Fliss said, trying not to laugh, "these things happen. Well, not to me, but…"

"You're married?" Bianca repeated.

"Yes," she said miserably. "But he said it was a terrible mistake. Which it was, of course. But then the plane crashed, and Mike died, and there was the funeral, and I was upset, so he came over, and we kind of… slept together. And then we did it twice more, and now I've fallen for him but he says he's not interested in a relationship so I told him to fuck off, and then Ian turned up, and now I don't know what to do."

"Holy shit," Phoebe said. "When you screw up, you really screw up, don't you?"

"So he's slept with you, but he's not interested in a relationship," Libby clarified.

Roberta nodded. "He won't explain why. I know he's hiding something from me. He says he's crazy about me, but that he can't commit right now. He's very secretive, and that's the last thing I need." She'd finished her wine and had a large mouthful of the vodka and tonic that Fliss had made for her. It was a relief to get it all off her chest.

"We had a big argument," she continued, "and I think it kind of ended things. And first of all, I thought well I don't need a man, I'm happy on my own, and I am, I really am."

"But…" Bianca prompted.

"But… if I'm honest with myself, I do want a family. I want a husband and children. For the first time I felt really broody. I've not felt like that before."

"I know," Libby said quietly. "I sometimes wonder if it's to do with approaching thirty. Tick-tock, you know?"

Roberta reached out a hand, and Libby took it. "Had you planned to have kids with Mike?" Roberta asked.

"Roberta!" Karen looked alarmed.

But Libby just smiled. "Actually, it's nice to be able to talk about it. Everyone's tiptoeing around me at the moment; it's just awful. Nobody wants to talk about him because they think they're going to upset me. And of course, I'm going to get upset, so they assume it's best just to not talk about him."

"Well that's bullshit," Roberta said, releasing her hand and pushing her drink toward her. "I don't care if you bawl your eyes out. You can say whatever you want with us. I'm not afraid of grief or any other sort of emotion."

Libby's eyes glistened. "You gals really are the best."

"I don't know what I would have done without you all after my accident," Phoebe admitted.

"How are you feeling?" Roberta asked her. "After the crash, I mean? It must have been twice as bad for you after your first accident and losing your memory."

"I'm okay." Phoebe was a little pale, her smile not as bright as it used to be. "But what you were saying about wanting kids… I've been feeling the same. It's such a weird, strong feeling. Rafe and I actually decided we'd start trying for a family when we got married, but we haven't had any luck so far."

Bianca hugged her sister. "It'll happen. It's only been five months and you've had such a stressful time."

"Yes, I'm sure you're right, although it worries me that the doctor said the accident I had might affect my fertility. But anyway, we weren't talking about me." Phoebe waved a hand. "So, Libs, had you and Mike talked about getting married and having kids?"

Libby pulled up her legs and wrapped her arms around them, resting her chin on her knees. She pressed her lips together, and gave them a sad smile and a little shake of her head as a tear ran down her cheek.

Roberta passed Libby a tissue from the box on the table. "You didn't, or you don't want to talk about it?"

Libby blew her nose. "He sort of got impatient when I tried to talk about it. The thing is…" She hesitated and glanced around at them. "We weren't in a great place when he… died. Things hadn't been good at home. We argued a lot, and he could be quite… mean…" More tears ran down her cheek. "I'm sorry, I shouldn't say things like that, not when he's gone…"

"Hey." Roberta moved across to hug her. "It's a terrible thing what happened, and we're all devastated that he died. But that doesn't make him a saint."

"Roberta!" Karen scolded again.

"Well, it doesn't. Libs, you're here with your friends, and you can say whatever you want to us. We're not going to judge you. No relationship is perfect."

"I know," Libby squeaked. "I just feel so guilty. It's okay, I'll be all right. Don't mind me." She wiped her face and had a large swallow of vodka. "I'm just going to get quietly drunk. You talk amongst yourselves."

"All right, sweetie." Roberta poured her another drink. She couldn't imagine what Libby was going through at the moment. If their relationship had been a bit rocky, it must really be making her all mixed up, she thought. Now probably wasn't the time to talk about it, with only days having passed since Mike's funeral. She'd let the dust settle, and then she'd talk to Libby about it again and see if she could find out a bit more.

"What about you and Elliot?" she asked Karen, remembering the way they'd seemed at odds at the party. "Do you guys talk about marriage and kids?"

"I've tried to. He just says he's not ready."

"For fuck's sake," Bianca said, "what's wrong with these men?"

Roberta shook her head. "I don't know whether they're afraid of committing themselves in case something better comes along, or it's a fear they're going to lose their freedom, or what."

"To be fair, Rafe never made me feel like that," Phoebe said.

"Dominic didn't either," Fliss admitted. "But then he's a bit older, and he's been married before, so I guess that's something to do with it."

"Elliot's hardly young," Karen said. "He's thirty in November, and I'm heading that way."

"I'm sure he'll come around soon," Roberta said, exasperated with her brother. "You want me to rough him up a bit for you?"

They all laughed, even Libby.

"You would as well," Karen said, amused.

"Damn straight."

"And you're changing the subject," Bianca pointed out. "Back to Angus and Ian. And the fact that you're married."

Roberta sighed. "I don't know, I'm all in a muddle. Seeing Ian again has really thrown me. It's been two years since we were together—if you can call it that—but I still have feelings for him. This was what I wanted, what I dreamed about for years. But now… I suppose I am worried he only wants me because he's alone. So maybe I don't believe he's the one who ended the marriage. And anyway, every time I think about him, I remember Angus, and I get all…" Her face grew hot.

The girls smiled. "Wow," Phoebe said softly, "you really have feelings for him."

Roberta swirled the vodka over the ice in her glass. "I do. And they're different from how I feel about Ian. I was so young when I met him, and he's older than me, more sophisticated. I hadn't had many partners, and he just blew my mind, I suppose. He was exciting, and if I'm honest, the fact that he was married gave it an edge, in the beginning, anyway. I'm ashamed of that now."

"We all make mistakes when we're young," Libby said. She scratched at a mark on the arm of the chair.

"Yeah," Bianca said, her lips twisting in a wry smile.

"What mistake did you make?" Phoebe asked her twin sister with surprise.

Bianca shrugged. "It wasn't a mistake so much as a missed opportunity, I suppose. When I was eighteen, I told someone I loved him. But he said although he had feelings for me, he wasn't ready to settle down, and he left."

"You're talking about Freddie," Roberta said softly. Freddie Brooks had been in the same year as Bianca and Phoebe at school, and he and Bianca had been good friends all the way through high school, although they'd never dated, to Roberta's knowledge. When he was eighteen, he'd joined the New Zealand Defence Force and had eventually been sent to the Middle East. He was still there, as far as she knew. "I didn't know you told him how you felt about him."

Bianca shrugged. "Water under the bridge now. I'm just saying we've all done it, made mistakes, or have things we regret."

Roberta felt a sweep of sadness for them all—for Libby, who'd lost her partner, for Bianca, who hadn't yet found her Mr. Right, for Karen, who was having trouble pinning down Elliot, for Phoebe, who was trying to get pregnant. Nobody's life was easy, she thought. Fliss and Dominic were possibly the happiest two of their group, but they'd both had to deal with issues to get where they were.

"So… which guy are you going to choose?" Phoebe asked.

"You should stay with Angus," Bianca said. "He's got a great job, and he was amazing on the plane. He's one of the good guys. Oh, and you're married, of course."

Roberta shot her a wry glance. "I don't think he's interested." The thought made her eyes sting, and she swallowed hard. "I suppose I'm afraid that if I say no to Ian, I won't meet anyone else, and then I've missed the chance to settle down and have a family."

"It's not a good enough reason to get back with him," Fliss said.

"I know." And she did. It would be a huge mistake for them to rekindle their relationship purely because they were both afraid of being alone.

"Do you still love him?" Fliss asked.

Roberta hesitated. "Not in the same way I did," she admitted eventually.

"And Angus?" Bianca prompted. "Do you love him? Your husband?"

Roberta's face grew warm. "It's too early to talk about love."

"But you're *in* love with him," Fliss said, smiling. "It's written all over your face when you talk about him."

"I don't know. I have feelings for him. But come on, in spite of the PJs, we're not fifteen anymore. We all know that a real relationship isn't just about having a crush on the guy. It's not all about sex. We have to think about whether he's reliable and honest and trustworthy, and oh my God I sound so fucking old."

They all burst out laughing. "But is he good in bed?" Libby asked impishly.

Roberta sighed and flopped back on the sofa. "Yes. Yes, *sooooo* good."

"Is he well endowed?" Karen asked, laughing when Fliss elbowed her. Phoebe coughed into her drink, and Bianca snorted.

"Actually, he's quite impressive," Roberta said. "Definitely a point in his favor."

They all giggled, and Fliss shook her head and poured them all another drink. The vodka was having an effect, Roberta thought. What had previously seemed disastrous now just seemed funny.

She took her glass from Fliss, feeling warm and contented, despite the troubles she was having. At least she had her friends.

They drank, ate the muffins and brownies, and talked about guys and sex and marriage as if they were all sixteen again, while Libby dozed in the chair, and outside, the moon rose slowly in the sky, watching over them all.

Chapter Twenty-One

It was Sunday afternoon, coming up for four o'clock, and Angus was on his way back to the Bay of Islands after his weekend visit to Auckland. There was still an hour or so until sunset, but the light was fading, and he'd already turned the car lights on.

He was nearing Whangarei—about an hour from home—when his phone beeped on the passenger seat, telling him he had a text. Seeing a Drive Thru' burger place ahead, he pulled in and ordered a cheeseburger and a coffee, and checked his phone while he waited for them to be made.

The text was from Elliot. It said, *Call in at Rafe's on the way home. We need to talk to you.*

He sighed. It was a long drive and he wanted to go straight home, pour himself a whisky, and get lost in one of his games for a while. Gaming was one of the few things he could do that didn't allow him to think, and he didn't particularly want to think at the moment.

He texted back. *Been a long day. I'll take a rain check and catch you tomoz.*

Almost immediately, Elliot came back. *Nope.*

Frowning at the curtness of both messages, Angus texted, *It wasn't a question.* Then he tossed the phone onto the seat and took his burger and coffee from the girl behind the kiosk.

He ate the burger as he drove, ignoring his phone, which pinged again three times before finally falling quiet. He didn't know what Elliot had up his butt, but he wasn't in the mood to be ordered around. It had been a trying few days. After Roberta had gotten out of the car, he'd driven to work in a temper, telling himself the best thing he could do was to forget about her.

He hadn't, of course. He'd thought about her non-stop, and had made himself miserable with the knowledge that she was almost certainly going to want nothing to do with him ever again, and rightly so, because he was an idiot.

She was better off without him, he'd told himself, and he deserved the pain and anguish he was going through. It was the price he paid for seducing her not once but three times, and for being incredibly weak.

And anyway, she was just a girl. Nothing special. Plenty more fish in the blah, blah, blah.

But of course, he was bullshitting himself, because she *was* special, and he was five kinds of a fool for trying to pretend she wasn't.

A trip down to Auckland had been the last thing he wanted, and it had been a difficult one, too, with Katrina in a pensive mood and baby Katie teething and demanding attention, and, quite frankly, he was glad to be on the way home.

So going six rounds with Elliot over something didn't appeal, and he drove past the turn-off for Rafe's house and instead carried on home, finally pulling onto his drive around five-thirty.

To his surprise, there were two cars there, and he sighed as he recognized both Elliot's and Rafe's. They got out as he turned off the engine, and he was surprised to see Phoebe with them.

"Hey," he said, walking up. "What's going on?"

"We need to talk," Elliot said. All three of them looked serious.

"I'm really tired," he said truthfully. "Can't this wait until tomorrow?"

"No," they all said together, so, frowning, he opened the front door and let them in.

"Coffee?" he asked, switching on the lights.

"No, thanks." Rafe led the way into the living room, and he and Phoebe sat on the sofa, while Elliot took one of the armchairs.

"For fuck's sake, what is this? An intervention?" He tossed his keys on the table and turned on the gas fire, starting to get cross.

"Kinda," Phoebe said.

"What?" Now he was confused.

"Roberta had a girls' night last night," Phoebe said.

He'd forgotten about that. "Oh, right."

"She told us, Angus. About Vegas. About the fact that she thinks the two of you are married."

He closed his eyes. "Fuck."

"Yeah," Elliot said. "Now, normally I wouldn't interfere in my sisters' love lives, but Rob's been through a tough time, and I think it's time I—"

"We're not married," Angus said, interrupting him.

Elliot's eyebrows rose. "*Ahhh…* what?"

Angus sank into the other armchair. "Well, what I mean is, the marriage is void. It's illegal. Because I'm already married."

There was a long, long silence.

"Well that took the wind out of my sails," Elliot said.

"Someone else you met in Vegas and handcuffed yourself to?" Rafe asked Angus.

"It's not funny." Phoebe sat on the edge of her seat with an angry frown. "What are you talking about?"

"I'm already married," Angus repeated. "It's a long story. But I've been shitting myself since Vegas because I've committed bigamy, and that's fucking illegal, and I could go to jail if anyone finds out. And not only that, but I've hurt Roberta, who's the one girl in the world I think I could actually be happy with, and now she hates my guts, so yeah, I'm a bit fucking stressed at the moment."

"Okay," Elliot said, "I might be able to help you out there."

"What do you mean?"

"You didn't marry Roberta," he said.

It was Angus's turn to get angry now. "What are you talking about?"

"We came back from the show," Elliot said, "and everyone went to bed, but I stayed in the bar to have a drink. When I came up, one of your shoes was caught in your door, so it was open a crack. I didn't want anyone going in and stealing any of your stuff, so I went to throw the shoe in and saw the two of you in bed. It was clear what had happened. So…" He scratched the back of his neck. "I thought it would be funny."

"You thought what would be funny?"

"I went down to the lobby, borrowed one of the hotel's computers, knocked up a fake marriage certificate, printed it out on their printer, and left it on the bed." He glared at Angus. "It had a fucking picture of Elvis on it. I thought you'd realize it was a fake."

Angus stood up, filled with horror. "It looked real!" He marched over to Elliot's chair. "You fucking idiot!"

"The witnesses' names were Lennon and McCartney," Elliot yelled, standing to face him. "I'm the idiot? Jesus Christ!"

"The thing is," Rafe interceded, stepping between them before blood was spilled, "he didn't tell any of us, and the next day the crash happened."

"I forgot," Elliot yelled. "I completely forgot about it." He ran his hands through his hair, and his anger died away. "I'm so fucking sorry."

Angus just stared at him. "So… we didn't get married?"

"No." Phoebe stood up and joined them. "You haven't broken the law, Angus."

He pursed his lips. "Actually, that's not strictly true."

"What do you mean?"

He sighed and sat back in the chair. The other three exchanged glances, then sat again too.

His head was spinning. He hadn't committed bigamy. That, at least, was something. He'd been racked with guilt ever since Vegas, unable to believe he'd done something so stupid.

There had been no ceremony, no exchanging of vows. He hadn't held her hand and promised to love her till death parted them.

Was it weird that he felt a twinge of sorrow about that?

"Angus," Elliot snapped, bringing his attention back to them.

"Sorry." He cleared his throat, sighed, and then began to tell them the sorry tale.

*

When he'd done, Phoebe covered her face with her hands. "This is such a mess."

"You're an idiot," Rafe told him.

"Tell me something I don't know," Angus said gloomily.

"You've got to tell her." Phoebe lowered her hands. "She knows something's up. You've got to explain it all to her."

"I will," he said. "I swear. It should all be sorted soon, and then I can come clean, and maybe—"

"No," Phoebe interrupted, "you don't understand. Ian came to see her yesterday."

He stared at her. "What?"

"He turned up about an hour before we all did. He told her that he's left his wife, and he wants her back. He's coming again tomorrow to talk it over with her."

Angus went cold. "Fuck."

"Yeah."

"She wouldn't go back to him though, would she?"

Elliot shrugged. "She's lonely, man. And she's approaching thirty. She wants a family and kids. And if the guy she used to love is standing there on her doorstep offering her that, I'd be surprised if she didn't at least think about it."

"She doesn't love him the way she used to," Phoebe said hastily, "she told us that. He hurt her badly, and even though he said he was the one who walked out of the marriage, I'm not sure she believes that. But I'm also not sure it matters. Like Elliot said, she's tired of being on her own. And, I hate to say it, but I think you've broken her heart a little bit. She's hurting, and Ian's offering her comfort. Can you blame her if she grabs it with both hands?"

Angus stood and walked over to the window. "No, I wouldn't blame her. She has a long history with this guy. This was what she wanted, wasn't it? For him to leave his wife." He felt as if a crushing weight sat on his chest. "I've slept with her three times—I can't compete with the love of her life."

"Jesus fucking Christ." Elliot stood up and ran his hands through his hair until it stuck up at right angles to his head. "I can't believe you. Is that it? Are you just going to roll over and accept it? Just let the bastard who cheated on his wife for five years and treated Rob like shit pretend everything's okay? Do you have any spine at all?"

"I hardly think you're the one to start pointing fingers, Mr. Photoshop," Angus snapped. "Sort out your own fucking relationship before you start playing a twisted Cupid to everyone else."

Elliot's eyes narrowed. "What's that supposed to mean?"

Angus rubbed a hand over his face. "Nothing. I'm tired."

"No, come on, the fucking gloves are coming off, and I want to hear what you've got to say."

"Elliot," Phoebe warned, and she and Rafe both stood up again.

Angus faced his friend, filled with hurt and anger at the unfairness of it all. "You and Karen are hardly Mr. and Mrs. Perfect, are you? Anyone with eyes can see you're not in love with her. She loves you, but you're just stringing her along because it means you don't have to be alone, and you get free sex whenever you want it. Do you think that makes you any less of a heel than me?"

"Angus!" Phoebe covered her mouth in horror. Rafe's eyes widened.

Elliot said nothing. He met Angus's eyes for a moment, his own so like his sister's, dark-green and surprisingly full of emotion.

Then he turned on his heel and walked out of the house.

"Elliot…" Angus called after him, but he shut the front door behind him, and within seconds they heard him start the engine, and the sound of tires scrunching on gravel.

Angus sank into the chair and put his head in his hands.

"Way to shit on your own doorstep," Rafe said. "Good luck with sorting that one out. Come on, Phoebes. Let's go."

"Wait." She came over to Angus and dropped to her haunches before him. "Go and see her. She's in love with you, you know. She wants you, not Ian. She'll understand, if you explain everything to her."

"She won't," he said hoarsely. "I've fucked everything up."

She pushed herself up, leaned forward, and to his surprise, kissed the top of his head. "You're a good guy, beneath all the idiocy. She knows that. Go and get the girl, Angus, before it's too late."

Then she turned around and left with Rafe, closing the door behind her.

Angus sat back in the chair and stared up at the ceiling. How could he have gotten it all so terribly wrong? He only ever meant to do good, but somehow he always screwed everything up.

Elliot hated him, and Roberta never wanted to see him again. He couldn't unsay the things he'd said; couldn't undo the things he'd done.

It was too late to do anything now about either of them.

Wasn't it?

Chapter Twenty-Two

Roberta sat at her kitchen table and pulled the A4 notepad toward her. She drew a line across the page with a ruler, dividing it in two, and then a line down the middle, dividing it into four.

Next, she wrote in one of the top boxes, *Ian—advantages,* and in the other, *Ian—disadvantages*. In the bottom left, she wrote: *Angus—advantages* and in the right, *Angus—disadvantages*.

Then she sat back and had a sip of coffee.

This could all be irrelevant, she told herself. For a start, Angus had made it clear that a relationship wasn't on the cards, so strictly speaking there was no decision to be made about him.

But that wasn't the point. She was trying to sort out her feelings about both men, and, as always, the best way for her to do that was to analyze everything and write it down.

She was going to start with Ian, she decided. First of all, advantages. She wrote down tall and good looking. Intelligent. Great cook, obviously. Witty. Good in bed. Generous with money.

She sucked the end of the pen for a bit. Should she put down loyal in the good or bad column? It had been loyalty to his wife that had stopped him leaving her, which was a good thing, from his wife's point of view. Bad for Roberta, though. And he'd hardly been loyal to her. She wrote it down in the bad column.

Next to it, she wrote dishonest, then added On so many levels. She pressed her lips together and wrote cheat, then weak. After that, she wrote shallow, impatient, and sometimes mean and cruel, as he'd often made fun of people, which she'd always disliked. Small hands, she added, because they'd always creeped her out a bit. Bad morning breath and also permanent coffee breath, because he drank a lot of it.

His negative column was getting a bit full now, but she hadn't finished yet. She wrote tennis, because while she didn't mind the game, he was obsessed with it, and talked for hours about who was playing in what tournament, which had bored her to tears. Garlic was next, because although he was a great cook, he added it to every meal. Aftershave, because he liked lemony scents, which she didn't. Nails, because he tended to wear them a bit too long for a man.

Now she was struggling to fit words in, but she still hadn't finished. She wrote snobbish, because he looked down on people who didn't wear designer labels with no thought as to whether they could afford it. Superior, because he laughed at those without a decent education. Arrogant, because whenever he'd visited her, he'd always assumed she'd put everything aside for him. Lastly, she wrote controlling. It was a hard word for her to use, because she considered herself a strong personality, and would have laughed in the face of anyone who said she was a pushover, but the truth was that he'd bought her apartment, her clothes, even her food at times, and she'd let him do it because she hadn't wanted to lose him.

There was no more room in the disadvantages column. She studied it, re-reading each of the words, frowning. She'd written so little in the advantages column. There had to be more, surely? But at the moment, she couldn't think of anything else.

Okay, so time to start on Angus.

She'd start with the advantages, as that was more fun. Would he have more or less than Ian? Physical first, she thought. Tall. Handsome—and she put a plus sign beside that, because he was better looking than Ian. Great build—with another plus, because Angus went to the gym often, and Ian didn't. Big hands, plus, plus. Short nails, plus, plus, plus. Nice feet—an odd thing to notice, but they were. Strong thighs. Gorgeous eyes. She hadn't commented on Ian's eyes at all.

All right, time to move on to other stuff otherwise she'd run out of room. So, what about his personality? Warm. Caring. Compassionate. Were they the same thing? No, not quite, so they both went in. Gentle—she liked that. Doctor, and a plus sign, because although it had been fun being with a chef, she preferred being with a doctor. She thought about the crash and wrote Brave. Intelligent. Hardworking. Calm. Firm. That made her smile.

What about when he was with her? Great in bed. That definitely deserved a plus sign, because although Ian had taught her a lot of things, Angus was a much better lover. She wrote tender. Passionate. Sweet. Sexy. Rough. She smiled again. Funny. Naughty. Kind.

She paused, then wrote love. Thought a moment. Then crossed it out.

His advantages box was full now, so she drew a bubble that extended it into the disadvantages area to give herself more space and added serious, because she liked that side of him, steady, reliable. And then she wrote hero, because he had been in many ways when they'd needed him on the plane.

She compared Ian's advantages column to Angus's. Jeez. Was there any area of Ian's that deserved a plus sign? Great cook, maybe, although Angus's Spanish omelet would have taken some beating, and he hadn't put garlic in it, which deserved a plus sign in itself.

All right, it was fine talking about all the good things, but what about Angus's disadvantages column?

She chewed the end of her pen and thought for a whole minute.

Okay, this was ridiculous. He wasn't perfect. He must have a heap of drawbacks.

But he wasn't vain, or impatient, and he didn't have a bad temper, that she'd seen anyway. He didn't go on about his work or his hobbies. Apparently, he couldn't hold his drink, but she didn't particularly see that as a drawback. She looked at Ian's disadvantages column, but couldn't apply any of them to Angus's; he wasn't arrogant, superior, or snobbish, and he wasn't mean or cruel, not in the least.

She wrote down the one fault she could think of: secretive. She believed he had feelings for her, but it frustrated her that he wouldn't tell her why they couldn't continue with a relationship.

Well, what a surprise. Anyone who looked at the piece of paper would be in no doubt as to which guy she should choose.

Not that she had a choice.

She sighed and doodled in the margin. It didn't mean the exercise was useless. What it had shown was what she'd known all along, really. Her relationship with Ian was done. She didn't want him back, not after all this time, and not after how he'd treated her in the past. She'd considered it because she was lonely and she wanted a family, but that wasn't a good enough reason to be with him. She'd known it in her heart, and this just cemented it.

Laying down her pen, she took a deep breath and let it out. She reached for her phone, thought for a while, then tapped out a text and sent it.

Then she poured herself a large shot of vodka.

She was just adding some ice to the tumbler when someone knocked on the door.

She stopped, startled. Fuck. It wasn't Ian, surely? Had he decided to come around earlier to try to push his luck?

At times like this, she wished she had a dog. Jasmine and Rosie were little use if a burglar had decided to pick on her. Mind you, burglars didn't normally knock. Even so, she picked up the umbrella she kept by the door, put the chain on, and opened it cautiously.

It was Angus.

"Oh." She blinked. He stood with his hands in the pockets of his jeans, the collar of his coat turned up against the cold wind. He looked tired, and had no smile for her.

"Can I come in?" he asked.

"Of course. Hold on." Her heart thudding, she closed the door and removed the chain, then opened it again. He stepped in, noticed the umbrella, and his lips curved up for the first time. "Is that in case I get out of hand?"

She gave him a wry look and put the umbrella back by the door. "I thought you might be a burglar."

"Burglars knock?"

"Yeah, I know. I'm a weak woman on her own; I have to protect myself."

"Ha! One thing I would never call you is weak."

She smiled and held out her hand. "Can I take your coat?"

He hesitated. "I don't want to assume I'm staying."

"You can always put it back on again."

"Fair enough." He slipped it off and gave it to her, and she hung it on a peg by the door.

He ran a hand through his ruffled hair, meeting her eyes. "Hey."

"Hey." She couldn't deny a deep sense of joy that he'd come to see her, but equally she had to be cautious here.

"I'm sorry I haven't called," he said, stuffing his hands back in his pockets. "I've been in Auckland—not that that's an excuse, I know."

She chewed her bottom lip. "I'd just poured myself a drink. I'm guessing you don't want anything alcoholic as you're driving, but would you like something else? Coffee?"

"Sure." He looked relieved that she was giving him time.

She gestured for him to follow her through to the kitchen. He sat at the table, and she began preparing the coffee machine. "It's a wild night to come out," she said. "It couldn't wait until tomorrow?"

"No. I needed to talk to you tonight."

"Okay." She blew out a long breath and slotted the capsule in the machine. What was this about? Please God, don't let him say *It's been great but I'm sorry, it's over…*

He didn't say anything else, so she waited for the machine to finish pouring the coffee, added a little milk, then turned to give it to him.

He was reading her list.

"Fuck!" She placed the coffee cup on the table and reached for the sheet of paper, but he held it out of her reach.

She folded her arms. "That's private."

"There's nothing in my disadvantages column," he said.

"I was just about to start that part when you knocked on the door," she said. "I left it until last because it's going to be the biggest one."

His lips twitched, and he glanced at the paper. "Under my advantages, you've written big cock."

She'd doodled it without thinking about it. "I had to make up a few things to fill the box."

"You've had to extend the box to make room for all my good points."

She gave up and sat down. "I was trying to sort my brain out."

His eyes took on a touch of pity. "I hear Ian came around."

"Who told you that?"

"I've just seen Phoebe."

She sighed. "Yeah."

He dropped his gaze back to the sheet of paper. "His disadvantages column is pretty big."

"Yeah, I know."

He scanned the sheet. "I get a plus for being great in bed?"

"Yes, Angus. You're the best lover I've had."

"I have nice feet?"

She sighed again. "What do you want?"

He put the paper down and leaned forward, elbows on knees, linking his hands. "I haven't been honest with you, and I want to change that now."

She frowned. "Did Phoebe prompt this?"

"In a way. She was waiting for me when I got home, with Rafe and Elliot. She'd told them what you'd said about us being married, and it turned out that Elliot had a confession."

She raised her eyebrows. "What do you mean?"

"He forged the marriage certificate."

She stared at him. "What marriage certificate?"

"Ours. In Vegas. Our door was open, and he saw us in bed and realized what must have happened, and thought it would be funny to make us think we'd tied the knot, only then the plane crashed and he forgot all about it."

Her jaw had dropped, her thoughts going around in her head as if they were on a carousel. "We're not married?"

"No." His gaze rose to meet hers.

Oh, what a sharp, sweet stab of disappointment that gave her. They weren't married. She wasn't his special someone, even if it was in name only. They weren't metaphysically bound together by some invisible twine; he wasn't her man, her one and only, the one she was supposed to be with. She wasn't going to be able to talk him into not getting divorced, because he'd never been hers anyway.

He dropped his gaze back to his hands. "Don't."

"Don't what?" Her voice came out sharper than she'd meant.

"Don't look so disappointed. I can't bear it."

She stood and walked away, folding her arms tightly across her chest. "I suppose you're feeling quite smug right now, aren't you? That's gotten you out of that little predicament."

"It's not like that."

"No? You told me it was all a terrible mistake, so it must be a huge relief for you."

"It's a relief, but not in the way you mean. I thought I'd broken the law, because I'm already married."

Chapter Twenty-Three

"Let me explain," Angus said.

"I think you'd better." Roberta's face had gone completely white.

He'd never forget her expression when he said they weren't married. She'd looked utterly devastated. She loved him, he thought—or at least, she was in love with him. She'd liked the idea of being tied to him, of being his girl.

He never, ever wanted her to look at him with that pain in her eyes again. He was going to sort this out if it was the last thing he did.

"Her name's Katrina," he said. "And she has a baby girl called Katie."

Sheer horror crossed Roberta's face. "You have a child?"

"No, no! Jesus, I'm fucking this up. No, Katie is Jamie's daughter."

She blinked a few times. "Your brother Jamie?"

"Yes. Jamie met Katrina when we were working in Belarus. Both her parents died when she was young, and she grew up in an orphanage. She was very young, very beautiful, and Jamie fell for her immediately. We were there for a year, and when it was time for us to go back to New Zealand, Jamie asked her to go with him, and she said yes."

Roberta didn't unfold her arms, but she looked a little less angry. "Did they marry?"

"No. They were going to. It was all arranged. She'd just found out she was pregnant, and then he died."

"Oh, jeez."

He sat back, exhausted from the memory and all the emotion. "She didn't have residency, and she had no qualifications or skills, so Immigration weren't going to let her stay. We started to look into a work permit, but of course she was pregnant, so she wasn't going to be able to keep working when the baby was due. Mum and Dad were devastated—they thought she was wonderful, and they were horrified

BRIDE IN SECRET

to think she was going to have to go back to Belarus and take their grandchild with her—their only remaining contact with Jamie."

"Did she want to go back?" Roberta asked.

"Not at all. She loved New Zealand and all the freedom we have here. Her country is beautiful in places but it's ruled by a dictator, and the government has been criticized for human rights violations. She'd just begun to make friends here, and she loved my parents, because of course she doesn't have any of her own. She was Jamie's girl, and she was about to have Jamie's baby. I couldn't bear to think his child was going to grow up on the other side of the world. So… I suggested we get married, and then she could apply for residency as my wife."

Roberta was quiet for a long time. Eventually, she lowered her arms and sat again. She had a long swallow from the glass of what looked like water but was probably vodka, he thought.

"So you thought you'd committed bigamy after Vegas," she said eventually. "That was why you were so worried about what we'd done."

"Yes."

"Doesn't it just make the marriage void, if you're already married?"

"Yes, but it's still illegal, and I could have gone to prison for it."

"You should have told me, Angus."

He ran a hand through his hair tiredly. "My marriage to Katrina is illegal too, in a way, as she received residency because of it. I was worried that if the authorities found out about the double marriage, they'd start looking into the marriage with her. The whole thing was a scary process. We had to prove to Immigration that we hadn't gotten married just to get her residency, so we had to produce evidence that we had a relationship, pictures of the two of us, that sort of thing."

"How did you do that?"

"I didn't sleep with her, if that's what you're asking. But we did live in the same house for a month before we got married. Separate bedrooms, I swear. We told everyone that we'd fallen in love after Jamie's death—Mum and Dad were the only ones who knew the truth. Katrina and I spent a lot of time learning about each other's pasts and our families, so we could pass any tests for Immigration. It was tough, but we did it, and she got her residency."

"So… you're still married to her?"

"At the moment. We decided to wait six months before I moved out, so it wasn't too obvious. I applied for the job up here. We count the day I moved out as the first day of our separation. The two years ends in September, and then we can start divorce proceedings."

Roberta's green eyes scanned him. "And in all that time, while you were living with her, you were never a couple?"

"Not in the Biblical sense. Never. She adored Jamie, and she missed him terribly. She had a tough pregnancy, and she suffered from post-natal depression after the baby was born. I helped out with Katie quite a bit, and Mum and Dad were always in and out. They help her financially, and I go down most weekends to see how she's doing. But she's improved a lot. She's got a job now, part-time in one of the local supermarkets, and Mum has Katie while she works. She has friends, other young mums, and they all support each other. She doesn't really need me now. I suppose I still go out of a sense of loyalty to Jamie, just to make sure his daughter is all right."

He looked across at Roberta. "Do you believe me?"

She nodded slowly. "Yes, I do."

He felt a wave of relief, and gave a long sigh. "I'm so glad."

"There's nothing else you haven't told me?" she asked. "Or any secrets that anyone else is keeping, for that matter?"

"Not that I know of. This is all of it. I'm so sorry about what happened in Vegas. I can't believe what Elliot did." He rubbed his forehead. "I was a bit harsh with him."

"In what way?"

"I told him to sort out his own relationship before he tried to sort out mine. I thought he was going to argue with me, but he just walked out."

Her lips twisted. "They say the truth hurts."

"Oh, you've noticed too?"

"Oh yeah. Karen told me that he won't discuss marriage or kids with her. I don't know what's going on there, but he's obviously unhappy."

"Jesus. Why's everything so fucked up?" He banged his fist on the table.

"Hey," she said, "I put calm in your list of advantages. Don't make me go and get an eraser."

He gave a short laugh and pulled the list toward him again. "Phoebe told me that Ian wants you back," he said, brushing his thumb over Roberta's looped handwriting.

"Did she now?"

"Has he really left his wife?"

She sighed. "So he says."

"Did he leave or did she throw him out?"

"Your guess is as good as mine. He seemed sincere. And it's the first time he's ever said anything about leaving, so it wouldn't surprise me if his marriage is over. But it's all irrelevant."

"What do you mean?"

"Look at the sheet, Angus. It's obvious that he's not the man for me. I stayed with him for a long time because I was afraid of being alone. But when I write it all out, it's clear that he has more bad than good points. He's not the man for me."

He swallowed and looked back at the sheet. "So what were you about to put in my disadvantages column?"

She took it from him and crossed out the word secretive. Then she wrote a few words and showed it to him. It said *Major pain in the arse*.

His lips curved up. "Is that it?"

"It's an over-arching description. It covers a hundred smaller things."

"Yeah, I get that." He reached out a hand and turned it over, palm up. She looked at it, then, to his relief, placed hers into it. "I'm sorry I didn't tell you before," he said softly. "After everything Katrina's gone through, I felt that I couldn't risk someone finding out that our marriage was fake. It wouldn't have been fair to her. Plus, of course, there's the risk of prison."

"Hmm. For a nice boy, you're quite the criminal mind."

"I know. Surprising, huh?" He stroked the back of her hand with his thumb. "I think it gives me an edge."

She rolled her eyes. "So where do we go from here?"

He lifted her hand and kissed her fingers. "Well, maybe we should start with… I want you. I know I don't deserve you, but I want you anyway. I've tried to kid myself that you're nothing special, but I know that's utter bullshit. I've never met anyone like you in my life, and I can't imagine I ever will again. You're one of a kind, an amazing woman, and I want you in my life."

She blinked, and her eyes glistened. "Say more nice things."

Joy filled him—he was winning. "Absolutely. I love your body, with your sexy curves. And I love the way your hair looks like melted chocolate when you've just washed it, and how it curls on my chest when you lay your head there and look up at me. I love your mischievous laugh, and your sense of fun, and the way you don't take any nonsense, not even from me."

"Angus…"

"I adore making love with you, and being inside you, and I want to be able to do that every day for the rest of my life."

"Angus…"

"I want to go to bed holding you, and wake up beside you forever. And I want to stand at the altar and tell everyone how much I love you and that I'm never going to leave your side. And then I want to have six children with you and watch you be a wonderful mother. I want to grow old with you, and watch your hair turn gray and wrinkle lines appear at the corner of your eyes, and know that you're mine, and no other man is ever going to lay hands on you again because if someone does, I swear I'll knock his teeth down his throat…"

"Angus!" Her bottom lip wobbled and tears tumbled over her lashes as she threw her arms around his neck. "Stop, stop!"

"I could talk forever," he said, lifting her onto his lap and holding her tightly. He'd never experienced such a swell of joy, and he buried his face in her hair, wanting to hold on to the moment that he realized he hadn't lost her, because it was oh, so sweet, like Christmas and his birthday and Valentine's Day all rolled into one.

"I can't believe it," she said, her voice muffled against his neck. "I can't believe you really want to be with me."

"Of course I want to be with you, you crazy woman. I promise to tell you that every day for the rest of your life. I love you so much."

"Oh Angus. We've only slept together three times. You couldn't possibly know that yet."

"I've been in love with you since the first time I saw you. You were always meant to be mine, sweetheart. It's written in the stars. Tell me I haven't got it all wrong. Tell me you want to be with me, too."

"I want to be with you." She took his face in her hands. "But first, I've got something to confess."

A flicker of doubt appeared inside him. "What?"

"When I tried to fill in your disadvantages column, I couldn't think of anything to put there."

The smile spread slowly across his face. "I think that's the nicest thing anyone's ever said to me."

"I mean it," she whispered. "I always thought you were kind and caring and honorable. What you've told me has only confirmed that.

I'm glad you helped your brother's wife. You're a special man, Angus, and I feel incredibly lucky to think you might be mine."

"I am yours." He gave her a fierce kiss. "One-hundred percent. And you're mine, Roberta Goldsmith. I don't care what's happened in the past, but from this moment on, you're mine, and if that wanker comes to your door again, I'm going to ring the fucking police and get Elliot to stick him in the cell for the night."

She laughed. "I think you would as well."

"I would." He tucked a strand of her hair behind her ear. "When are you going to tell him he's not welcome here anymore?"

"I already did." She reached out and got her phone, swept her thumb across the screen, pressed a few buttons, then showed him a text she'd sent. It said, *I've made up my mind, and we're over, Ian. Don't bother coming back tomorrow, because I won't let you in. We're done.*

She lowered the phone to the table. "Okay?"

He nodded slowly. She'd told Ian it was over before he, Angus, had come around. That gave him a glow all the way through. "Okay."

She cupped his face again and stroked his cheeks with her thumbs. "Will you stay the night with me?"

His brow furrowed, and he touched his nose to hers. "Are you sure?"

"I'm sure."

He pressed his lips to hers. "Then yes. Of course."

Chapter Twenty-Four

They locked up the house, and Roberta directed Angus to go to bed while she went into the bathroom.

She brushed her teeth, but she was so full of emotion that it was hard to swallow, and her eyes stung. His story had touched her heart, and even though she wished he'd told her earlier, she kind of liked the fact that he'd wanted to keep Katrina's secret out of loyalty to her and to his brother. He was an honorable man, and there weren't many of them around nowadays.

I've been in love with you since the first time I saw you. You were always meant to be mine, sweetheart. It's written in the stars.

They were such beautiful words. She looked at herself in the mirror, wondering what he saw in her, what marked her out as special in his eyes. She couldn't believe that the man she'd liked for so long was saying them to her. She felt like Cinderella, when the prince turns up on her doorstep with the lost shoe, or Sleeping Beauty, after being kissed awake.

She supposed that she deserved a fairytale ending as much as anyone. And it felt odd, as if she'd won the lottery. So many people across the world failed to find love. So many love stories ended in heartache. Was hers really going to end in fireworks and a ride off into the sunset?

After turning off the light, she left the room and went into the bedroom, leaving the door open a crack for the cats to come in later. Angus sat in bed, his back against the pillows, reading a piece of paper. She put her hands on her hips as she realized it was the list she'd written earlier.

"Strong thighs?" he commented. He lifted the duvet and looked under it. "I guess."

Giving him a wry look, she undressed and slipped beneath the duvet. "Give me that."

He held it out of her reach. "It fascinates me."

"Why?" She tried to grab it, and he moved it away again.

"Because it's not often you get a written record of everything your girl likes about you. I still can't get over the fact that you like my feet."

"What's not to like? They're very nice feet. Quite big. And you know what they say…"

"Yes, you've written that down, too. You really think it's big?"

"Angus…"

"You wrote hero," he said.

She gave up trying to get the paper and lay back with a sigh. "What you did on the plane was very heroic. I think that might have been the moment I fell in love with you."

"I was only doing my job."

"Even so." She smiled.

He looked back at the paper. "You wrote love and crossed it out."

"I didn't want to presume."

"You also wrote rough. You like it rough?"

"Will you please put the paper down?"

"You've also put gentle. Way to confuse a guy."

"Jesus." She snatched it out of his grasp and tossed it on the floor.

He chuckled, held her wrist, and pulled her on top of him. "Got you," he murmured.

To her shock, her eyes filled with tears.

His eyes widened, and he cupped her face. "Hey, what did I say?"

"Nothing, nothing…"

"Sweetheart…" He kissed her, so tenderly it made the tears even worse. "Aw, come on. Don't cry."

"I'm sorry."

He lifted her off him and pulled her into his arms. "Come here."

She curled up against him, fighting the wave of emotion that refused to go away. "I'm sorry," she squeaked again. "I hate crying."

"What's the matter?"

"It's just been a tough few weeks, a real rollercoaster, and I knew you liked me, but I thought I'd lost you…"

"You'll never lose me," he whispered, and kissed her again, his mouth moving slowly across hers.

She let him kiss her, but the tears wouldn't stop, and eventually he sighed. Stretching out on his side, facing her, he brushed under her eyes with his thumb.

"Can I meet Katrina?" she asked.

He looked surprised. "Oh. You want to?"

"She's important to you. I think I should."

"Then of course. We can go down next weekend, if you want."

"I'd like that. Do you think she'll like me?"

His lips curved up. "How could she not?"

"I mean it. I haven't met any of your family."

"I'll take you to meet my parents," he said. "I've told them so much about you, so they'll be thrilled to meet you at last."

"You've told them about me?"

"Of course. And Katrina. She's been insisting for ages that I should tell you about her."

"Really?" That surprised her. "She's not… jealous?"

"Jealous? God, no. She'll be glad to see the back of me."

"I doubt that," Roberta said softly. "I'm surprised she's never asked you if you'd like to stay married."

He tucked a finger beneath her chin and lifted her eyes to meet his. "Is that what's worrying you? Katrina has no feelings for me in that way, I swear. She's a dear friend, like a sister. We talked for a long time about getting married, because both of us hold the institution in high regard, and neither of us liked the idea of making a mockery of it. We did it because there was no other option. And I'm glad I did it—I wouldn't change a thing. It was the right thing to do, morally. But I'm sorry for the fact that it has cast a shadow over the two of us. I'd do anything to take that away."

Roberta shook her head. "There's no shadow, I swear."

"You're the only woman for me. You don't know what agony it's been watching you from afar all this time, trying to tell myself that I couldn't have you. When I married Katrina, I decided to throw myself into my work and that I wouldn't get serious about anyone until the two years was up. And on the first week I moved to Kerikeri, I met you. I couldn't believe it. I knew as soon as you walked into the bar that I was going to have trouble."

"I thought you didn't like me much," she whispered. "You never seemed interested."

"I'm so sorry." He kissed her. "I'm going to make it up to you every day for the rest of our lives. I swear."

"I'll hold you to that," she said, and lifted her lips for his kiss.

*

Eight days later

"So what was she like?" Bianca asked.

It was late Monday afternoon, and the mad rush of customers in both the Bay of Islands Brides shop and the Bridal Café had finally died down. Roberta's sisters had come into the café with their mother for a well-earned latte and one of Roberta's new Spanish omelet muffins, inspired by a certain handsome GP. Libby brought their coffees over and joined them for a moment, as the café was quiet.

Roberta had told them all about Angus's marriage to Katrina, and the day before, she'd finally gone down to meet both her and his parents.

"She was lovely," she said sincerely. "Beautiful and exotic, with a strong accent. And little Katie was gorgeous."

"Was she... friendly?" Phoebe asked. Roberta had expressed her secret fear that she'd meet Katrina and see in her eyes that she was secretly in love with Angus.

"Very friendly," she told them. "It was obvious that they knew each other well, but there wasn't a hint of anything but a kind of sibling affection between them. And while I was there, she told him that she's met someone. He's the manager of the supermarket where she works. They've been out on a couple of dates, and she had real stars in her eyes. She was obviously worried that Angus would be upset because she was finally moving on from Jamie, but of course he wasn't, he was just glad that she's finally found someone."

And relieved, she thought, although she didn't add that. She thought that, deep down, Angus had been concerned about divorcing Katrina and leaving her to fend for herself; not because she was weak and feeble, but because he felt he owed his brother more than that. So even though Roberta knew he must feel sad to think that Jamie's girl was moving on, it had come as a relief to him that someone else would be taking over responsibility for her.

"So when can they file for divorce?" Noelle asked, sipping her latte.

"September. Angus reckons it'll all be done by Christmas, so..." Roberta blushed. "He wants us to get married in January."

Wonder lit their faces and they all cheered and came over to hug her.

"Oh my God!" Phoebe squealed, "I can't believe it!"

"I want you to make the dress," Roberta told her sisters, blinking away her tears.

"Of course!" Bianca threw her arms around her. "We'll make it the best dress ever!"

Roberta squeezed her back, then turned to give Libby a hug.

"I'm so pleased for you," Libby whispered.

"Thank you." Roberta could only imagine how hard it must be for Libby to say that after losing her own partner.

Finally, she turned to her mother, and Noelle gave her a big hug, saying, "That's wonderful news."

"I can't believe how much has changed in such a short time," Roberta said, wiping her eyes. "Not long ago, I thought I was destined to remain single forever."

"Phoebe mentioned that Ian called again," Noelle said.

Roberta nodded. He'd rung after he'd gotten her text, begging her to reconsider and have him back, and although she'd insisted he leave her alone, he'd called again the following Friday. Angus had been there, and to her surprise, when he'd realized who was on the phone, he'd held out his hand to talk to him. Although she'd felt perfectly capable of dealing with her ex, she'd handed the phone over more from curiosity at what he was going to say than anything else. Angus had told Ian firmly that he'd asked Roberta to marry him and they'd set a date for the New Year, and if Ian rang her again, he'd personally drive down to Auckland and shove the phone somewhere the sun didn't shine. Angus had hung up and given her a somewhat apologetic look, but she'd just burst out laughing.

"He won't ring again," she just said with a smile.

"I'm glad." Noelle looked so relieved that Roberta could tell she'd been worried that her daughter would be drawn back to the guy who'd broken her heart.

"And here's the man of the day!" Bianca said with a smile as the door jangled.

They all turned, and Roberta's heart swelled as Angus entered and everyone cheered. He grinned and walked up to them, put his arm around Roberta, and gave her a quick kiss.

"She's just told us about the wedding," Noelle said. She reached up and kissed his cheek. "I'm so glad."

"Just doing what I was told," he said, and winked at her.

"So where are you two going to live?" Libby asked.

"Oh… um… we haven't talked about that yet," Roberta said, her face growing hot.

"Well, we'll leave you to catch up," Noelle said. "Come on girls. Let's close up the shop."

They left the café, and Libby collected the cups and took them back into the kitchen.

Angus took Roberta's hand, and led her over to the window. The sun was low in the sky, filling the high street with a deep orange light. The temperature was dropping, making Roberta think of cuddling up in front of the open fire with him. If they went to her place, that was. Over the past week, they'd spent more time at hers because of the cats, but as much as she loved her home, she couldn't assume he would want to make it his full-time residence.

"She raises a good point," he murmured, resting his hands on her waist. "Have you given it any thought?"

She gave a shy shrug. "I don't know how you feel. You might want your own space from time to time."

"It's hard enough being apart from you during the day; I don't like being away from you at night." He kissed her nose. "I have a suggestion to make. If you want to move in with me, that would be wonderful. If you want us both to sell and buy a joint place, that would be fine, too. But… I know how much you love your house. You've worked so hard on your garden, and you have that amazing kitchen. So… if there's room in it for me… Shall I move in with you?"

A huge smile spread across her face. "Do you mean that?"

"Of course I do." He lifted his hands to cup her face and kissed her. "I want you to have everything you desire. I want you to be the happiest woman in the world."

"I already am," she whispered. "But yes, I'd love you to move in with me."

He wrapped his arms around her, and she lifted hers around his neck. "I can't believe I'm getting married."

"I don't know what you think," he said, "but I wondered whether you'd like to get married in Dominic's church."

She moved back to look at him, her jaw dropping. "Seriously?"

"We could talk to him and see what he thinks. Obviously, I'll have been married before, so I don't know whether that would be a factor. And it's a long time since I've been to church. But because marrying Katrina was like a business contract, and after the debacle in Vegas, I'd like to do it properly. To swear in front of God and our friends and family that I'll love you forever."

"I love you," she squeaked.

He lifted her chin and smiled. "I love you too." And then he kissed her, filling her heart with joy.

Newsletter

If you'd like to be informed when my next book is available, you can sign up for my mailing list on my website, http://www.serenitywoodsromance.com

I also send exclusive short stories and sometimes free books!

About the Author

Serenity Woods lives in the sub-tropical Northland of New Zealand with her wonderful husband and gorgeous teenage son. She writes hot and sultry contemporary romances. She would much rather immerse herself in reading or writing romance than do the dusting and ironing, which is why it's not a great idea to pop round if you have any allergies.

Website: http://www.serenitywoodsromance.com
Facebook: http://www.facebook.com/serenitywoodsromance
Twitter: https://twitter.com/Serenity_Woods

Printed in Great Britain
by Amazon